The Utterly Uninteresting & Unadventurous Tales of Fred, The Vampire Accountant

THE UTTERLY UNINTERESTING AND UNADVENTUROUS TALES OF FRED, THE VAMPIRE ACCOUNTANT

Drew Hayes

The Utterly Uninteresting and Unadventurous Tale of Fred, the Vampire Accountant

Cover design by Ashley Ruggirello
Cover art Copyright 2014 hjoranna/StooStock/theRomancee/withmycamera/Giallo86/freetextures/Falln-Stock on DeviantArt.com and book image courtesy of jaysonhome.com

ISBN: 978-0-9896499-9-5

REUTS Publications
www.REUTS.com

THIS BOOK IS DEDICATED TO THE UNCOOL, UNCOORDINATED, UNEXCEPTIONAL, UNCHARMING, UNINTERESTING, AND ESPECIALLY THE UNASHAMED. TO EVERYONE FROM THE AWKWARDS TO THE ZEROES, LIVING AS THE PROUD ODDBALLS THEY ARE. THIS BOOK IS DEDICATED TO MY PEOPLE.

PREFACE

I ALMOST CERTAINLY DO NOT KNOW YOU; however, I shall assume you are a lovely person, and it is my loss for not having the opportunity to meet you. Still, I must assume you and I are connected in some way, for the works you are about to read are selections from a journal of my memoirs. I compiled these not in the belief that the stories within are so compelling they must be told, but rather because I found my unexpected life transition to be so shockingly uneventful—at least initially. I place the blame for my aggrandized expectations squarely on contemporary media, filling my head with the belief that a ticket to the supernatural also put one on an express train toward coolness and suave charm.

This is simply not the case. Or, at least, it was not my case. I recorded my journeys in the hopes that, should another being find themselves utterly depressed at the humdrum personality still saddling their supernatural frame, they might find solace in knowing they are not the only one to have felt that way. Given the lengthy lifespan of many of the people with whom I associate, there is no guarantee they will have passed on by the time this is read. Therefore, names have been changed as I deemed necessary.

So, dear reader, whom I suspect is a wonderful person merely in need of a bit of reassurance, take comfort in my tales of uneventful blundering. One's nature is hard to change; sometimes even death is insufficient to accomplish such a task. But be assured that, while you might find yourself still more human than anticipated, you are far from the only one. You will eventually discover that under the movie stereotypes, imposed mystique, and overall inflated expectations, each and every one of us is at least a touch more boring than our images would indicate.

And that is not a bad thing.

-Fredrick Frankford Fletcher

A VAMPIRE AT THE REUNION

1.

I WAS MIDWAY THROUGH PACKING WHEN I paused to contemplate whether it was appropriate to bring the blood. I mean, sure I needed it and all, but there's always been something so garish about pulling a bag of O Negative from my little leather luggage. I weighed the options for a few moments, pitting my desire for stylish secrecy against my nutritional needs. In the end, I forged a compromise, pouring the blood into my faux silver (obviously the real deal is off limits) flask, sealing it well, and then placing it between my freshly pressed shirts.

My name is Fredrick Frankford Fletcher, and yes, that name did get me beaten up quite frequently when I was a child. For those of you who are a little slow on the uptake, I am also a vampire. A relatively recent life change. It happened only about one year ago. I'll spare you the gory details, but one night I was a mild-mannered accountant with a heartbeat, and the next night I wasn't. Oh, I was still a mild-mannered accountant, but the heartbeat was long gone. I took it well, I feel, or as well as one can handle such things. I attempted to go hunting and feed; however, while I might have been a fearful predator of the night, I still chafed at the idea of physical violence. I can't even watch slasher films without covering my eyes. After a few failed feeding fiascos left me leaning toward starvation, I opted to use a different set of my skills to secure sustenance.

John Smith, as I will call him here, was a local hospital director that had paid me to cook his books and keep his failing enterprise above water in previous years. Generally, all criminal activity gives me ulcers, but the cause of keeping a hospital afloat allowed me to feel that the karmic scales balanced out. After my life change, we struck a new deal: I would offer the same service each year in exchange for the opportunity to purchase my dinners of choice from his blood supply.

The rest of my lifestyle adaptations were fairly simple. I began having files delivered to my home so I could work on them at night, I refitted my refrigerator for a predominantly liquid diet, and I resumed my life as it was. I was even able to continue indulging my penchant for fine cheeses, despite what voluminous lore had told me. Without being crass, let me simply say an undead body handles normal food as a human one handles gum. While not built for nourishment, it is capable of disposing of such materials. A fact that was far from the first discrepancy I'd uncovered in my cinema-based education.

Perhaps if I'd had any true friends or family, the transition would have been more difficult; however, that was not a burden with which I had been shouldered. My life was just as gray and dull as it had been before.

In a way, that was the most difficult part—going from the thrill of something new to the dreariness of the old. I suppose a part of me had believed the Hollywood hype about vampires living (in a non-literal sense, of course) adventurous lives filled with sex, danger, and riches. My own undead experience had been . . . somewhat less thrilling. I've spent ample time raiding the video stores in my town, and I must say I have yet to uncover any tales of vampires whose unlives continue so perfectly parallel to their days of breathing and sunshine as mine has. I would have taken great comfort in such a film. It was that nagging sense of disappointment that toiled away in my subconscious and it was the need for something—anything really—to be different that prompted me to make such a dangerous decision.

I was going to my ten-year high school reunion. Now, I know that this must seem like an impulsive and idiotic idea, and, in truth, it was. I saw that clearly when the invitation arrived. I recognized it, analyzed it, and catalogued it in my mental filing system as I had done with everything else in my monotonous twenty-eight years on this earth. This time though, something caught on the corner of my cranial cabinet, and I saw an opportunity. Here was a chance to take a risk, albeit a small one, and do something that qualified as unsafe. Whimsical even, if one discounted my previous analysis of the situation. Before I could talk myself out of it, I mailed my confirmation reply and booked a non-refundable ticket to my hometown of Kent, Idaho. It was only later that I realized the flight was scheduled during the day and was therefore useless to me, but the grandness of the gesture remained poignant, and I resolved to attend my reunion anyway.

Some three weeks later, as I packed up my supplies for the weekend to come, I began to wonder if other vampires felt skittish before seeing people who had known them in life. The only other vampire I had even encountered was the one who turned me, and he was gone before I awoke. I prowled the darkness at first, hoping to find others of my kind, but after a few movies depicting the vampire political system, I started staying in more. I didn't really have the constitution for such constant subterfuge and betrayal. A pleasant evening with merlot, blood, and brie worked just fine, thank you very much.

I zipped up my bag and hefted it onto my shoulder. This would have been an ordeal in itself three years ago, but with the night hours and the new allergies to garlic, silver, and sunshine came a few undeniable perks. The enhanced strength, durability, and dexterity were all quite nice. I was more than a minor klutz in my human days, so it was an enjoyable change to walk around without injuring myself. Eternal life was pleasant enough I suppose, though I'd become concerned about what I would do once I finished viewing every movie in the rental store. At least I might be around long enough to truly enjoy the appreciation of my smarter financial investments.

After locking my door and setting my alarms, I stepped into the new-night air. It was crisp with the chill of late October. Admittedly a strange time for a high school reunion, but Kent was a farming community. The fall holidays were close to harvest time, and therefore the heaviest celebrated. (For those of you fortunate enough to not understand that reference, harvest is one of the hardest working periods on a farm. A night off is not just reason to celebrate; it is reason to celebrate to the umpteenth degree. Since Thanksgiving is spent with family, Kent will often hold its reunions on or around Halloween.) This year was my class's turn, and as Halloween fell on a Saturday, our event was planned for the night of the pumpkin-themed holiday. As a real live vampire would be in attendance, I felt this was particularly appropriate. Even if I was the only one who would know it.

I loaded my leather suitcase into the back of my gray hybrid. I had always tried to be eco-conscious, but realizing that I could actually live to be affected by eventual environmental disasters had doubled my efforts. Once the suitcase was secured, I placed a travel mug of blood into the cup holder and buckled myself in as well. I would have to drive through the night to make it to my hotel in time, but that hadn't been an issue for over a year. If I were still human, I would have taken a deep breath to steel myself for the expected adventure ahead. Since I was not, I checked my mirrors and turned on my signal, pulling into the road with both hands firmly on the wheel.

2.

I MADE IT TO THE HOTEL APPROXIMATELY an hour before the sun would crest the western horizon. Almanacs were never something I gave much thought to before my change. Now, they were like credit cards; I never went anywhere without one.

Check-in was a simple process. One advantage of my timing was that none of the other alumni would be entering. They had either come earlier or would be showing up during the day. That was well and good for me; I had neither desire nor intention of seeing them outside of the controlled environment the reunion would offer. Less chance of anyone remembering favorite old games of beating me up or throwing me naked into the girls' locker room that way. Just the memories would have given me a stress headache, if I were still susceptible to them.

I received my key packet from a girl working the front counter and ventured up to my room. Once there, I opened my suitcase and pulled out my safety materials. I had several rolls of tinfoil and tape. It took me twenty minutes to seal off every possible avenue the sun might utilize to enter my room—a skill sheer survival had forced me to practice at length.

I gently removed my costume from the suitcase and began shaking out the obvious wrinkles. Yes, since we were having the reunion on Halloween, it had been designated a costume party. My costume was a set of scrubs and a white doctor's coat. Now, I'm sure some of you will wonder why I didn't simply throw on black clothing and bill myself as a vampire. The sad truth was that I looked precious little like an undead demon of the night. Granted, the dying had slimmed me down and taken away my need for glasses, but I still had the same mousy brown hair, round face, and unappealing arrangement of features I'd always been cursed with. I'd already favored a pale complexion, so that difference was scarcely noticeable. My fangs only extended themselves if I was feeding, exceptionally hungry, or . . . um . . . ah . . . otherwise excited, to put it properly. It also didn't help that almost immediately after the change, I took to wearing fake glasses with similar frames. It might not seem rational, but after twenty-five years, they were as much a part of my face as the eyes they stood in front of, and I couldn't bear to part with them.

All of that reasoning aside, the point of a Halloween costume is to be something you are not. Since I was (and am) a vampire, that would have been cheating. At least, that's how I rationalized it to myself as I ironed my costume and hung it in the hotel closet. I did a few shirts next, making certain I would have appropriate clothing to wear on my return drive Sunday night. There was really no rush; I had gotten a week ahead on my work so that I could spend a few more days here if the desire struck me. I couldn't possibly conceive of a reason why that desire would strike me—I had left this town as fast as my awkward human legs would carry me—but it was my understanding that impulsive people were given to inclinations such as that. This weekend, if never again, I was determined to be impulsive. Or as impulsive as a vampire with four clean pairs of clothes and a four-day supply of blood can be.

I settled into the bed and turned on the television. (Contrary to popular mythology, I neither sleep in a coffin, nor am I rendered powerless during the daytime. The difference between the two is that in the daytime

I can sleep, which is an ability I lack under starlight. I don't have to, and in fact spent three weeks without any rest during last year's tax season; however, I am a creature of habit as much as of the night. I slept my whole life. And I saw no compelling reason to change that in my undead incarnation.) I clicked through the channels until I was satisfied that there was nothing worth staying up for, and then set my alarm for 5 o'clock sharp, putting in a wake-up call for the same time. The reunion began at 7 p.m., and sunset was at 7:17 p.m. This way, I had ample time to shower, get into my costume, and enjoy some blood before heading into the night. I didn't really need to drink every night; twice a week would serve my needs quite well. However, I have a tendency to stress eat, which caused my human form to become somewhat doughy. The effects weren't quite so negative this time. I simply increased my blood bill for the month.

I could tell the sun had risen by the time on my clock. My foil shielding had worked flawlessly; not a speck of light leaked through. With a minor expenditure of effort, I pushed my mind away from consciousness and into what was, I assumed, the vampiric equivalent of a REM cycle.

3.

I MUST ADMIT, MY FORMER ACADEMIC colleagues were quite adept and varied in their costume conceptions. The only rules of the evening were that one could not cover one's face—which apparently served to fuel the creative fires in fashioning a functional costume—and that a visible nametag was required all night. The latter of those two killed any sense of realism I might have felt while staring at Anne Boleyn, Elvis, or Jake Blues. However, my doctor garb was relatively untainted by the cheap tag. I had read the invitation carefully and had therefore procured the name-badge holder that real doctors use to slip the identifying piece of plastic inside. There are times when it pays to be careful and prepared.

As I slunk, for lack of a better word, around the cheaply decorated cafeteria, I found myself taken aback at the changes that had clearly not taken place in my fellow Kent High alumni. Near the entrance sat a fairy princess in a low-cut top: Joyce Trainer, homecoming queen turned mother of four. To the human eye, she appeared a miracle, still firm, fit, and perky even after four rounds with hormones and weight gain. She was significantly less miraculous to me, since I could actually smell the plastic and Botox that riddled her body. Ah, the crux of vanity. The upside of never having good looks was that I didn't have to fear losing them with age. Pity I wasn't pretty though; they would have kept for eternity then. Although, for all I know, I wouldn't have been bitten if I were good-looking, so I suppose there's no sense second-guessing fate.

Brent Colter, one of many of my school-day bullies, was standing near the refreshment table, romancing a collection of former co-eds whose names I couldn't recall. His cheap Spartan costume covered him fully, but it was tight enough that his frame was hardly obscured. His former football-player's physique had softened around the edges, but as the ladies' attention indicated, he was still a broad-shouldered, muscular man. I felt mildly disappointed; I was hoping he would have devolved into full blown obesity, but I suppose ten years is a little soon to expect age to have caught up to him so severely. It dawned on me that I wouldn't be able to attend many more of these. Sooner or later, someone would notice that the rest of the class was growing older, while dear Fredrick stayed frozen in his mid-twenties. Brent was clearly aging though, which was pleasant to see in my former tormentor. I was hopeful that I could visit him in the nursing home one day and rub in that I was still young and fit while he had grown weak and decrepit. Assuming I could find time to keep track of him, of course . . . and only if I could be assured he wouldn't spill my secret to others . . . and if it wasn't during tax season.

Maybe I would just settle for a trip to dance on his grave.

The nameless clustered herd of my class was filled with people who were as much the same as they were different. Bodies had grown or shrunken with mass and minds had been filled by knowledge or numbed by boredom, but the people under the faces were nearly the same as before. The basketball team was dressed predominantly as pimps and rowdily slapped high fives with each member to enter the gym. The chess club was in their own corner, dressed in superhero costumes that bore exceptional detail. The theater club was here and there, dressed as characters I could only half recognize from famous plays and films. Amidst it all, I felt just as I had in my human days—different and set apart. I took a seat at an unoccupied table, sipping on the poorly flavored sugar water they had the gall to call punch. I should have been up and mingling, but that just wasn't me. I wasn't like these people . . . even back when I was still biologically like these people.

I was on the verge of giving the whole trip up for a bad idea when the devil sat down next to me. She was wearing a black and red corset, with black leather pants and red boots. Two horns sprouted from the blonde hair that hung to her shoulders; red contacts obscured the brown eyes that I could still make out underneath. She was fit and sexy. Not a whiff of plastic on her person, either. A vampire in the movies would have delivered the perfect opening line that conveyed mystery, power, and sex appeal.

Instead I said, "You're supposed to be wearing a nametag."

She arched an eyebrow and stared me down for a few moments. I had begun contemplating whether or not to fake a bathroom emergency to escape when she replied, "Well, I am the ultimate rebel."

I laughed a little in spite of myself. I liked rules, and they only worked if they applied to everyone, but I also liked a beautiful woman who would talk to me. Guess which one was taking precedence at that point?

"Seriously though," I said, "how do we know who you are if you aren't wearing a nametag?"

The devil leaned toward me, offering a more apt view down her corset in the process, and whispered conspiratorially, "And why do you want to know who I am, doctor?"

"Well . . . um . . . I suppose we might have known each other . . . back when we went to school here."

"Did you know many women who looked like me?" she asked with a hint of purr in her voice. All her body language indicated that she was flirting with me, but her heart rate was steady, and I didn't smell any pheromones or hormones being released. If only I'd had these senses during my formative years, I could have saved myself a multitude of embarrassments when girls thought it was funny to flirt with the nerd.

I pulled my back straight and made a significant effort not to look down the appealing ravine of her corset, and then spoke. "I feel I knew far too many women like you in those days. Granted, none bore your particular physical features, but the streak of cruel humor was most notably the same. I don't know why you are pretending to flirt with me, but I assure you that I am on to your little game. I would very much like it if you left me alone now."

If I were still human, my face would have been bright red from embarrassment. I expected her to be grumpy that I'd spoiled her fun, or at least fake anger at me for calling her out. The devil did neither. She threw her head back and laughed wholeheartedly. I became increasingly uncomfortable as she devolved into guffaws and then chuckles. Finally, when her humor was little more than a low murmur in her throat, she responded.

"Well look at you, Freddy. Ten years and about fifty pounds ago, you never could have stood up to a girl like that."

I blinked a few times (another trait that is all habit with zero need) before tentatively answering, "Krystal?"

Krystal was the only female friend I had in my younger days, and, truthfully, saying "friend" is stretching it. We were both out of shape and had more caution than ambition in the social world. We didn't really spend time together per se, but our friend group was the same, so we knew one another well enough. She had an annoying habit of nicknaming people, so I was thusly deemed "Freddy" in her eyes.

"You got it, Freddy, and in one try too. I think I should be a little bit offended." She smiled at me as she reached into her purse and pulled out her nametag, sticking it in a very high-profile area on her corset.

"Wh . . . what . . . what on earth happened to you?"

"About the same as happened to you, I'm sure. Lasik for my eyes, diet and exercise for the body, just plain old growing up for the rest. You look good, by the way, very lean."

"Thank you," I murmured. I was glad I didn't have blood pumping through my system anymore, otherwise I would have been so red-faced my costume could have been titled "Dr. Tomato."

"So catch me up, Freddy. How has life been? What do you do? You have a wife?" She began blathering, eschewing the calm and seductive vibe.

"Life has been . . . well, pretty boring, to be honest. I work as a CPA. No wife or girlfriend, but I do have a very robust film collection. Yourself?"

"Eh, not so far off from yours. No relationships . . . they don't work so well with my line of work. I can't say my life is boring, but it is more predictable than I would like sometimes. All in all not too bad though. I make a living, and that's something to be thankful for."

"True. So what is it that you do?"

"Ahhhh, what now?" She tripped over her words as her heart rate went up. I had just caught her off guard.

"You mentioned your job was counter to relationships, but didn't clarify what it was. Therefore, I asked what your job was."

"Oh. I'm a . . . cosmetologist. You wouldn't believe the hours they make us work. No time for dates at all. Look, Freddy, I need to use the ladies' room. I'll be back in a few minutes," she lied. I turned my attention back to my glass of punch as she hustled herself off to the restroom. If I'd thought I wanted to leave earlier, getting recognized and then ditched by one of the few people I'd thought of as close to a friend had undoubtedly strengthened that resolve.

I left my sad little corner and ventured to the refreshment table. Brent was still talking to two girls—one a slutty cop and one a slutty nurse—but otherwise the area was unattended. They detached themselves from him and headed toward the restroom. With the looks they were throwing back, it was not at all likely that he was being abandoned in the same fashion as me. It wasn't even eight yet, so the party was relatively sparse. I had been led to understand that it was more fashionable to arrive later, but it was a talent I never had the inclination or the opportunity to cultivate. After all, the few times I'd been invited places, I was too afraid of missing things to arrive late, and I was too tired to stay when things worth seeing actually happened. I blended into the background, and no one ever remembered to invite me a second time. As I took a small block of swiss onto my plate and refilled my punch glass, I began thinking that maybe it had been better that way. At least at home I was comfortable. Being out here, with these people, I was just being reminded of all the things I wasn't. And alive wasn't even the highest item on the list.

I stayed in my funk until an hour later, when the lights went out and the chaos began.

4.

THE CROWD HAD SWOLLEN WITH COSTUMED former students. The range and variety of outfits was actually rather fascinating. Everything from vampires and werewolves, to pixies, knights, and what I was ninety percent sure was a local fast-food chain's mascot. I had plucked up enough courage to speak to a couple of people whose names I vaguely remembered, though my attempts were not well received. There had been a select few I would have been comfortable talking with, but, unfortunately, aside from Krystal and me, none of the formerly socially outcast individuals had elected to attend. I had kept an eye (and perhaps a nose) out for Krystal; however, she seemed to have utterly vanished since her trip to the ladies' room. I was standing by the gym's bleachers, fighting with myself on whether staying or leaving would be more cowardly, when the power in the building suddenly died.

At first, there was an awkward chuckle that rippled through the attendees. Power outages happen, and when they do, it is human nature to assume that someone is already on the problem fixing it. I scarcely even noticed. I didn't need light to see. After a few minutes, some of the more responsible members of my former class elected to open the doors and let in light from outside. That was their intention, anyway. I heard the rattling from the door frame and recognized the sound even before the shout of clarification accompanied it.

"Hey . . . hey! This isn't funny. Somebody locked us in!"

I was remarking in my mind how much more at ease I felt with everyone as invisible as me when a second scream tore through the party, this one much bloodier than the original. Everyone turned in the direction of the yell, but I'd bet I was the only one who could actually see a pudgy brunette mummy being pulled into the hall-way. I was sure I was the only one who could smell the sweet, tangy blood pouring across her sadly appropriate bandages. And odds were good I was *still* the only one who could make out the form of the hulking creature in the doorframe that was doing the dragging. All of this told me quite clearly that being at this party was no longer a minor risk. In that moment, I decided to do what any intelligent vampire would do in my position.

I ran like hell.

Admittedly, I jumped the gun before the rest of the revelers, but they had only heard a horrific scream. I had seen what caused it. They joined in a few seconds later, though. Say what you will about humans; they have a flight-or-fight instinct that is surprisingly well developed. They didn't even know what was going on, and they were making the right move.

Or were they?

I slowed my sprint to the door and moved toward the side of the wall. The rest of the crowd assaulted every exit, only to find each one reinforced and wrapped in chains on the outside. I could have ripped them down if it came to it, but then I would have had to explain how I did it once we were outside. Being hunted as a monster by a group of angry townsfolk wasn't much better than the situation I was already in, so that was a last resort.

There were two other ways out of the gym. Doors leading into the school were located at both the north and south ends. Since the scream had come from the north, everyone began stampeding toward the south exit. As I watched them, I was struck by how much they resembled livestock being herded into a chute. That thought solidified my decision. No way was I leaving with the crowd. I could just wait until they all left and then rip open a door and be on my merry way. I know it seems like I was being a coward, but let's be fair. These were hardly people I had fuzzy feelings toward, and dying scared me quite a bit more since I had already done it once.

I was watching them stumble over ill-conceived costume decisions as they fumbled in the dark when something caught my eye. There was a commentator's box near the top of the gym. It had a catwalk and opened into the second floor of the school. With all the bleachers pulled out, it would be easy enough to access; however, since they were shoved into the wall, it would be nearly impossible to reach from here. That is, assuming one didn't have enhanced physical abilities and a fear that served as an exceptional motivator. It was pitch dark, and no one was looking at me anyway.

I scaled the bleacher wall in under a minute. If anyone noticed sounds from the room behind them, they opted not to try and peer into the darkness, but rather to just escape faster. The door on the side of the commentator's box was unlocked, so I slipped in without needing to break off the handle. From here, it would be an easy journey to an outside balcony where I could hop down to my car and safety. I was halfway through the small cube when a surprising scent caressed my nostrils. Leather, human, sweat—and recent familiarity. Krystal. Now that I was listening, I could hear her heartbeat as well. She was bound and gagged, taped under the table where the commentators would normally sit.

I reached her very quickly. Helping a former friend was all well and good, but I still needed to get the hell out of there. She immediately began thrashing against her bonds and screaming into her gag. I'd forgotten I was the only one of us who could see in the dark.

"Krystal, calm down. It's Fred. Something very strange is happening, and I'm trying to get you out of here." She stopped struggling immediately and looked in my direction with gratitude and what seemed like a bit of embarrassment. I released her from the table's underside with relative ease. The tape was a more gradual process, but once I freed her arms, she was able to help the escape effort.

"What happened to you?" I asked as she spit the last fibers of her gag from her mouth.

"I got ambushed in the bathroom. Stupid bitches."

"Ambushed? By whom? Why would they do that? What the hell is going on? Do you know why the power's out?" My frustration at the evening's sudden turn from unenjoyable to potentially deadly apparently decided to manifest itself in the form of verbal diarrhea. Under my articulated assault, Krystal's heart rate spiked again, and then subsided. Her face took on a resigned look. Much the way it had when we were kids and she was on a diet. She might not like what she was about to do, but she would do it anyway.

"Okay, Freddy, slow down. I owe you a little bit of truth for helping me out tonight. I gotta keep it brief, though; this isn't exactly the safest area to hide, since it's the first place anyone who wants me will look."

"That's fair." In reality, her point made me far less concerned with my own ignorance of the situation and more interested in extricating myself from it. However, I was genuinely curious, and Krystal was still wearing her corset. Besides, if push came to shove, I would probably be okay. Vampires can really haul some ass when needed.

"To begin with, I'm sorry I flaked out when you asked me about my job."

"It's okay, Krystal."

"Nah, it isn't. You're a sweet guy, Freddy, and I know how personally you take that kind of stuff. See, I didn't actually come here planning to talk with anyone tonight, but when I saw you sitting by your lonesome, I couldn't help myself. Then you caught me off guard with the job thing, and I didn't have a lie prepared."

"So, why did you come tonight, if you weren't going to talk with anyone?" As I asked my question, she began rooting around the room blindly, groping under chairs and in cabinets.

"I came here on assignment for work."

"Will you elaborate this time?"

She let out a heavy sigh. "Dammit, Freddy, this is the kinda shit I was specifically trying to avoid. Look, I'll tell you what I do, but you won't believe me." She had finished the obvious places and began checking behind speakers and electronic equipment.

"Given that I just found you bound and gagged, my mind is somewhat more receptive than it might normally be."

"Well, then, here's the deal," Krystal said as she sat down next to me. "Everything you think you know about monsters is a lie. Ghouls, ghosts, werewolves, all of them and more are real and hiding out behind the scenes in our world. Officially, they are known as 'parahumans,' and part of my job is to hunt down the ones that get out of hand. I work for an agency without an official name or address. And I'm here because we learned that some local werewolves planned on using tonight as an all-you-can-eat buffet. You know, you can call me crazy at any point here and I'll shut up."

"What about vampires?" I asked. From the look on her face, that was hardly the response she was expecting.

"Um, yeah. Vampires are real too. They're hard as shit to root out, though, and major league badasses to boot. Only the top operatives deal with those things."

"I see," I said. I was a little relieved. If they thought that highly of vampires, it was unlikely I'd have to deal with this "agency" anytime soon.

"I gotta tell you here, Freddy. You're taking this a hell of a lot better than I was expecting," Krystal said, before resuming her hand-guided search around the room.

"It's been an interesting few years. Besides, as I said, finding you stuffed under a table lends some credence to your story. What are you looking for anyway?"

"My purse. I need my gun and silver bullets. I thought I heard them put it in here somewhere, but I didn't really have a great vantage point, so I might be wrong."

I could feel my skin prickle at the mention of silver. Still, if she was going to gun down several monsters, she would need her weapon. I smelled carefully, trying to ignore her immediate scent. I needed to track the same smell, but a version that was muddled and fading. That would lead me to any objects that had spent prolonged amounts of time around her, such as her purse. It took me only a few seconds to find it; the kidnappers had oh-so-cleverly put it inside one of the speakers. I got up to pull the speaker open, but a power cord had entangled my foot. So instead, I went crashing into it head first.

"Shit!" Krystal whisper-shouted. "Are you okay?"

"Fine. Just fine. Cheap plastic, and all that. Also, I think I found your purse." I handed it to her as I pulled myself up and extricated my leg from the diabolical power cord.

"Awesome! You still rock, Freddy." She pulled a handgun from the purse, followed by a series of clips exuding a smell that made my stomach start churning. She tucked all of it into her pants, then pulled out what appeared to be a pair of swimmer's goggles with electronics glued to them. She adjusted the band and slipped them over her eyes. When she turned to me and waved, the gears clicked in my head and I realized she was wearing extremely compact night vision goggles. I also realized I should probably pretend to be far less capable of seeing in darkness than I really was.

"Thanks for the assist, Freddy. You literally saved some lives tonight. Once this is all said and done, we should get lunch or something before we head home."

"Sounds like a pleasant way to spend an afternoon."

"Yeah." She went to the door that led into the school's second floor, pressing her ear against it and keeping her gun at the ready. Her free hand crept down to the knob, turning it slowly until it came to an abrupt stop. "Damn, it's still locked." Her head flicked toward me for a moment. Then she took a knee and produced a set of picks from her hair. In seconds she had the lock disabled and had resumed her careful opening of the door. She pulled it inward inch by inch, minimizing the sound and getting a full view of the hallway. After stepping out to make sure it was clear, she walked over to me.

"Okay, Freddy, listen close. The nearest balcony is to your right. Once you walk out the door, go right 'til you hit a wall, and then go to the left. Trace your hand along the wall on your right, and when you feel the third door, open it. It should be a classroom with a big window and door to an outside balcony. I know it will hurt, but you need to jump off that balcony and run to your car. Roll with the landing if you can—it will minimize the chances you'll break something. You got all that?"

"I believe I can handle it."

"Good. One last thing" —she pushed a stiff, smooth rectangle into my hand— "that's my card with my cell number. Give me a call when you're safe, and let me know you lived through this. Okay?"

"I certainly will," I lied.

She got up and headed back to the door. Gun in front, she exited, pausing only to look at me once more. I remembered that I wasn't supposed to be able to see those looks, which then made them all the more curious. At any rate, I was ready to get out of there. Krystal had handed me an exit, and I had no inclination to let that information go to waste. I'm sure a Hollywood vampire would have run after her, swept her into his arms, and handled all the villains himself. That, however, was not me. All I wanted to do was get back to my hotel room safely and relax.

Werewolves, real or not, most definitely fell into the realm of someone else's problem.

5.

STARING DOWN FROM MY HIDING PLACE ON the balcony, I discovered that, actually, the werewolves fell squarely into the realm of my problem. There were three of them patrolling the parking lot; three sedan-sized mounds of fur and muscle, with teeth that looked as though they could tear through metal. They were staying low among the vehicles, visible only from a higher vantage point. So far two separate groups of humans had made it to the parking lot, only to be struck down before they could get near their cars. The werewolves weren't killing yet, just subduing. Every so often a howl would echo from the school's interior, and the sentries would perk their ears. I could only guess at the messages being conveyed.

I was lying flat on the balcony, watching the scene from a nearby window's reflection. None of the options placed before me were appealing. I could vault the balcony and make a run for it, hope to stay here until the werewolves moved on, or sneak back into the school. The problem was that I didn't know if I could outrun these things. If I stayed here till sunup, I'd be dead anyway, and from the sounds inside, it seemed like other werewolves were working their way through the building. Once they caught my scent, I'd have no hope of hiding out. The heavy padding that arose from down the hall—behind my hiding spot—made my decision for me. At least with a running sprint, I'd have the advantage of surprise.

I shot upward and leapt the balcony's railing in a single motion. On pure instinct, I rolled with the landing and promptly cursed myself for wasting time instead of hitting the ground running. I recovered quickly and took off through the lot. I kept my speed within human limits to start. I might only get one chance to outrun or maneuver these things, and I didn't want to give them any warning of what I could really do.

A pair of werewolves rushed from the parking lot's entrance, trying to pincer me from both sides. They angled themselves diagonally, blocking the lanes to the left and right, and prepared to charge if I tried to go around them. I must admit, these things were far smarter than mere animals. The only options they had left me with were to fruitlessly try to dodge and get torn to pieces or run smack into the grill of the pickup truck in front of me.

I chose the latter. I jumped atop the truck and bounded over its roof without breaking stride. If you have never been fortunate enough to see a look of utter surprise race across a werewolf's face, I highly recommend you do so. My furry foes were forced to backpedal and change directions, getting into the rows on either side of me. No doubt they expected me to disembark from the truck and give them a chase on the ground. Their hopes were dashed when I vaulted directly from the truck onto the next car in line and kept running. Going from car to car would have been hard for humans, but not impossible. They would have had to be exceptionally well balanced and in excellent shape to use the strategy at a full run, though. In life, I was neither of those things; however, now, I was rather happily enjoying my undead advantage.

The chase continued across several lanes of parked cars. A few times, one of my pursuers would try to mount a vehicle in hopes of overtaking me on higher ground, but their vast size and weight always made the footing unstable. They contented themselves with snapping at my heels, never quite snaring me but doing considerable damage to the metal beneath my feet. I sincerely hoped everyone who made it out of here was insured. Speed-wise, they were able to keep pace with me, unfortunately. The upside was that I could move faster than this if I needed, and while they would tire out eventually, I was under no such limitation. I allowed a cautious amount of optimism to creep over me. Once I tuckered these two out, I could make an earnest break for my car and escape. It seemed like I was going to be okay.

In keeping with the ways of the universe, though, it was at that moment I was run over by a third werewolf. I was so preoccupied with handling the two below me that I had forgotten there was another to watch for. He slammed into me from his hiding place in the bed of a nearby truck and hurled me from my position. I crunched into a motorcycle a few yards away and lay there. A hit like that would have easily incapacitated a human, and as far as these things knew, that's what I was.

The one who hit me—a gray beast whose size seemed closer to the bear family than the wolf one—came over and sniffed. I kept myself still as death, which is ironically quite difficult for me. Just because my body doesn't have to move doesn't mean my consciousness doesn't want to. The only concession I made was to move my chest up and down, making sure they all knew I was still "breathing." A sharp tug on my leg let me know they were dragging me to wherever they had taken the others. I kept my eyes closed and my false breathing steady.

My therapist says I have confrontation issues. He's not wrong. At least, he better not be at his prices. As I lay there, being dragged toward who knew what, my thoughts were not on fighting my way free or saving the rest of the class. No, my mind was in my apartment in Winslow, Colorado—all those miles away—fervently trying to think of a way to get back there.

6.

BY THE TIME I FELT LIKE IT WAS SAFE TO "wake up," I had been blindfolded and tied to a metal bar in—of all places—the gym. I couldn't see anything through my black-fabric blindness, but I could smell the fear and blood coming from all my fellow victims. It seemed like nearly all of us were here, and from the sounds of struggling, they were just as restrained as I was. Four figures were moving around freely, though: two of them on four feet, and two of them as bipeds. There was no talking: only barks and snarling. In the far distance,

I could vaguely make out the sounds of someone drawing closer to our location. Part of me hoped Krystal was coming to help out, but part of me wished she would just see it was hopeless and leave. She had been kind to me that night, reminding me of the few people I had liked and trusted in my living days. I didn't want to see her get killed in some pointless attempt to save us.

A loud, booming voice interrupted my attempts to track the approaching figure.

"Ten years!" It echoed. "Ten years since our pack was formed. Ten years in secret. Ten years in silence. Ten years in darkness!"

It sounded familiar. Guttural and with a canine undertone, but familiar nonetheless. It continued, "You have all come here to reunite over what you once were, while we have come to see the last you will ever be. Tonight, we no longer hunt in secret! Tonight, we force the world to see and accept us for the superior species we are!"

The voice I might never have placed; however, the ego shone through crystal clear. Brent Colter. Looks like my old bully had traded up in the world. No wonder he was still so muscular and strong. Doesn't it figure? I become an undead creature of the night, and I can't even get a date. He becomes a glorified mutt, and he manages to pull off a grand murder plot. Jerk.

"Tonight, we sacrifice all these souls to our goddess, Grwlbrkgrwl (Look, I'm doing my best to be accurate here, but if you know a way to transcribe a name whose pronunciation sounds like nails in a garbage disposal, I'd love to see it), who will bless us with the strength to overcome all who stand against us. Then, we shall spread our strength until it is the humans who hide and live in fear, and never again the True Wolves!" Howls of what I assumed was agreement followed Brent's speech.

The bonds holding me in place were suddenly severed, though the ones binding my hands were left intact as I was pulled into the air by rough, coarse hands. A tug tore away my blindfold, affording me a full view of my surroundings. The party atmosphere had been largely wrecked by the mad trample for the doors. Tables and chairs were overturned, streamers and bits of costume littered the floor, and unclaimed nametags were scattered like confetti that yearned to be identified. In the center of the room now stood a small platform, and atop it a metal framing with straps for holding appendages. The roof had been opened, and moonlight was spilling down onto the new platform, illuminating the series of blades and blunt instruments attached to it.

My fellow classmates were all bound to the bleachers, arms tied together so they had no hope of getting free. They were blindfolded as well. It made a bit of somber sense—give someone a feeling of fear, and they get passive. Let them know inescapable death is at hand, and they'll fight with every measure of strength they have.

The hands holding me in the air did indeed belong to Brent, though they were much bigger than normal. He stood below me, half in wolf form, half in human. He was at least seven feet tall, covered in shaggy black hair, and his face was contorted into a hideous partial muzzle. The other two werewolves from the parking lot were still in full fuzzball mode, though the gray wolf had shifted into a form similar to Brent's. I didn't recognize who the gray wolf was, but I'd had a voice and personality to help me figure out Brent's identity.

Brent smiled, I think, and his voice rumbled.

"Well, well, well . . . Faggy Freddy came back for the reunion, huh? I can't think of a better person to start with." With that, he tossed me over his shoulder and began sauntering slowly toward what I had already come to think of as the Death Rack. He took his time, moving with a rhythmic precision that I can only assume was part of the ceremony. Panic was welling up in me, and it was looking more and more like my only chance to escape would be showing my nature and making a dash for it. As I looked at my old classmates, though, my constant plan of flight faltered. These people weren't ones I particularly cared about; however, it still sickened me that they were lined up like cattle waiting to be slaughtered. In fact, that's exactly what they were. As I stared at them, I began wondering what kind of lives they had, what families would miss them when they were gone. Sure, I'd coped with my death easily, but my life hadn't been that great to begin with. I hadn't had anyone who would miss me. All of this bounced around my skull during Brent's slow march toward the Death Rack, my eyes trained on all these helpless people. And then, staring at them made me realize something entirely different.

They were all blindfolded. Which meant they couldn't see me. Which meant that, for the next ten seconds or so, I was free of the rack and there were no human witnesses. I darted my gaze around, desperately searching for something I could use to turn this situation in my favor. We were halfway to the rack when I saw what I was looking for. It would be close, but I had a shot. Brent continued moving forward in that strange, faltering manner. When we were only a few steps away, I sprang to life (so to speak). I snapped the cords tying my arms, pushed off Brent's shoulder, and knocked him off balance. I'd had a feeling he wouldn't let go. Thankfully, I was able to stagger him enough to make a diving lean for my target.

As I look back, it seems like there were a number of options available to me. I could have grabbed a plank off the bleacher wall and cracked it into my adversary's spine, I could have sunk my fangs into his arms and ripped myself free, or I could have used my strength to punch him in the head. I didn't do any of those things. The problem with all of those solutions is that I was never a violent person, and a few death and near-death situations weren't going to change that. I was still me. So, instead, I took advantage of the fact that the Kent party planning committee had anticipated all foreseeable (or so they thought) emergencies.

I pulled myself to the wall and chomped down on a fire extinguisher. I don't know if this is something you've ever had occasion to do; however, I recommend against it unless you have a vampire's jaws and body temperature, because that stuff comes out fast, and it comes out cold. In seconds, a white mist had filled the air around me, coating everything with the slick, white, flame-dousing foam. I said a silent "thank you" that it was a full-size model and not a dinky miniature, and then wriggled free of Brent's grip in the confusion, taking care once I hit the ground due to its slipperiness. From the startled yelps and sounds of impact, it seemed that the werewolves couldn't maneuver so well in these conditions.

I felt Brent shift from beside me and rear back. By the time his fist struck the wall, I was on his opposite side. It took only a well-timed shove to send him sprawling to the ground where he scuttled about, trying to get footing. I must say I took extreme pleasure in that part. The initial mist was already clearing, though the white foam was going nowhere, so I capitalized on the chance to free my fellow classmates.

I didn't bother freeing their hands; instead, I pulled a knife from a nearby gladiator costume and began cutting the cords that held them to the wall. Tearing off their blindfolds as I went left them free to escape if they wanted, albeit their hands were still tied in the matter. (Heh, heh. Get it?)

They were funneling out the door to the south, and I was making good progress, but the werewolves were regaining their footing. I was only a quarter of the way through, and it began to look like that was all I would get done. The whole pack was in pure wolf-form now, and with four feet on the ground and no mist in the eyes, they were rising like the tide from that cold, damp floor. I'd done all I could do, and now my only choices were to free as many as I could before they attacked or run like the hounds of hell were chasing me . . . which, I suppose, they were.

I flipped over the knife in my hand a few times and swallowed out of habit. No more clever justifications or stall tactics left, no way to convince myself the people I left behind would find their own way out. Anyone I left here would undoubtedly die. Painfully. Whatever I did now, I'd have to live with for the rest of my unlife. I looked at the four behemoth killing machines advancing toward me, and then at the shivering humans helplessly lined up along the wall.

I made my decision.

That's when the gunshots rang out.

7.

"YOU WERE REALLY WAITING BACK IN THE commentator's box that whole time?" I asked.

"Well, not the whole time," Krystal said. "I saw them take you down, so I followed where they brought you. The box had been trashed, and I figured they'd realized I was gone. It seemed like the best place to be was the one I knew they wouldn't look." She poured five packets of sugar into her coffee, followed by at least three creamer packets. Stirring without spilling was shaping up to be an ordeal.

Krystal and I, still in costume no less, were sitting in a small all-night diner a few miles away from the high school. It was 3 a.m., and the emergency vehicles could still be seen heading to and fro along the highway.

"I have to wonder, what will the official story be on this?" I said as she began slurping down her diabetes in a cup.

"Mental breakdown by charismatic former athlete prompted him to create a murder cult." Her words came between rapid gulps of the steaming beverage.

"And our part in it?"

"Never happened. Local law enforcement responded with quick, surgical precision and averted a potential catastrophe. Sadly, the cult members were unwilling to listen to reason and had to be brought down. Two men on the force will be getting promotions."

I shook my head. "You don't think the two men receiving these rewards will be a little suspicious?"

"I think that this happens more than you might expect, and that the men who receive them will be chosen because they are either too dumb or too smart to question it."

Our conversation was cut short by the doddering waitress finally arriving with our food. Egg white omelet for me; waffles and bacon for Krystal. (I lectured her for at least five minutes on cholesterol after she ordered.) We dug into our food, but my eating was more for appearance's sake. I'd taken a healthy draw from my flask while driving over, so I was quite full after the night's festivities. We dined in peace for a few minutes. Then Krystal spoke up midway through the food, words slurred and muffled by her syrup-slathered batter morsels.

"So, when did you die anyway?" she asked. I started to choke on my omelet, then remembered I didn't need to breathe. I swallowed the lump down slowly.

"I have no idea what you mean."

"Sure you do. You're a vampire." She neither looked at me nor slowed her intake while making her accusations. Impressive.

"I'm an accountant, Krystal, though tonight I was costumed as a doctor. I live alone in my two-bedroom apartment and watch a lot of movies in my free time. Nothing about me really screams vampire." As I finished my rebuttal, she took a long draw from her coffee cup. Putting it down, she wiped her mouth and pushed her food to the side. She locked eyes with me.

"Fact number one: you rescued me in a room where the door to the corridor was locked, which means your only way in was to scale the wall. You did so without making any noise, or I would have noticed. Fact two: you were one of the most skeptical people I ever knew, and yet when I told you the world was full of monsters, all you wanted was information on a single type of them. Fact three: I tailed you after you left the commentator's box and watched your little circus show on top of the cars. You've never been even remotely athletic or coordinated enough to pull anything like that off. Fact four: you jerked free of a werewolf and bit through a damn fire extinguisher. Despite what you might think, I'm good at my job, and you're not very practiced at hiding your nature. Now, will you give it up and just answer my question so I can keep eating?" She cocked an eyebrow, waiting for me to respond. I motioned for her to go ahead, and she began shoveling her food again.

"It's nothing too exciting. I got grabbed off the street about a year ago and fainted from the shock. When I woke up, I was like this."

"Kept the same job, huh?"

"Yes. I like what I do, and I didn't see any reason to give it up."

"Makes sense. Want to go out tomorrow night?"

"*What*?" In my defense, I didn't have a lot of experience with beautiful women asking me out. She took it in stride.

"You're a nice guy. We've got a good history. Plus, you aren't that hard on the eyes. And you actually know what I do for a living. Do you know how nice it will be to go out with a guy I don't have to keep lying to?"

I mulled it over. "How do you know I'm not a bad vampire? What if I'm the kind you have to hunt down?"

"You aren't. I called in your plates while I drove over here. You've got a spotless reputation. A pretty boring one, actually." She gave me a wink, a grin tugging at her mouth.

And there it was. My unlife was so boring that even the woman who hunted monsters saw me as harmless. The one risk I had taken had backfired horribly. I wound up chased, beaten, and nearly killed by werewolves.

But, then again, I was sitting across from a very good-looking woman who was asking me on a date. Maybe my first risk hadn't played out so badly in the end. Maybe it was time for another. After all, I did still have four days of clean clothes and blood. Plenty of time to schedule some spontaneity.

"I'll pick you up after sunset," I told her, mustering all my courage and including what I hoped was a flirtatious smile with my invitation.

A ZOMBIE AT THE LARP

1.

THE MORNING AFTER BEING TURNED INTO a vampire, I instantly knew some things were going to have to change. I would no longer be able to make it into work at the accounting firm, I would have to forgo any walks in the sunshine, and I would need to get used to a far more liquid-based diet. These were things I understood and accepted with a humble grace. What I did not expect was that the accounting business I'd started to accommodate my new lifestyle would explode with popularity.

At a time when most people were making plans for the upcoming Thanksgiving holiday, I was working around the clock, trying to meet deadlines for all the new clients I had recently acquired. I'm not exaggerating, either. At night, I can take enough Percocet to kill a bear and still be wide-eyed. In the day, however, the mystical forces that animate my now dead body relent and allow me to slip into slumber. But under the sudden rush of work, I'd been awake for three nights and days straight.

It was really my own fault. When I returned from my high school reunion, I came back to a mountain of new assignments that had arrived in my absence. I could have turned some of them down, of course, but that would have involved talking on the phone—and possibly yelling or shouting—and the truth is, I'm just not very good at confrontations.

Now, I know what you're thinking. Who ever heard of a vampire that was scared of conflict? Well, I was non-confrontational in life, so I am still non-confrontational in death. Yes, we vampires are portrayed as a group of, for lack of a better term, "badasses," but as far as I can tell, we are greatly similar to who we were when our hearts still beat, only with paler skin and more physical prowess.

I clapped a pair of documents together and joined them with a paperclip as I let out a sigh. (Yes, I can still sigh, and I still make a habit of taking in oxygen with my lungs, though I do not know if it still qualifies as breathing at this point.) I was nearing the end of this week's work, but I still had hours of filing and data entry left. It was tedious work that required no special skills and was usually outsourced to temps or assistants. Since I had neither and suspected none would be willing to work with someone of my . . . condition, the grunt work fell firmly on my own narrow shoulders.

I went to the fridge and pulled out a plastic thermos, then popped it in the microwave. It was ready after a few minutes, and I all but cannonballed it. I overeat when stressed, you'll recall, but with all this work, it will be easy to afford the extra blood. I could always cut that cost, in theory, but my few attempts at feedings were less than spectacular. The last of those excursions—a pitiful effort capping off a string of failures—began with trying to skulk along a rooftop as I trailed a lone pedestrian, followed by tripping on loose brick and cracking myself in the mouth, and ending with me taking a tumble into a nearby apartment's dumpster. That's when I learned the downside of vampire senses, along with the fact that the building in question hosted an unusually large number of babies still in diapers. There was no dry-cleaning that smell from a pair of khakis.

Dabbing my mouth with one of my black napkins (you can only imagine the stains I got when I still used white ones), I washed out my thermos and began heading back to my desk. I worked in my apartment, which was windowless and possessed excellent security. I had all work sent and returned via a courier service, ensuring I could lead the lifestyle I desired in the privacy I loved. Aside from the courier, there were only a few people who knew my address, and my apartment complex was not the sort where uninvited guests could saunter in to talk to the residents about religion or the incredible savings opportunity they were presenting to a select few.

Which is why the thundering knock on my door garnered such a severe and shocked reaction; I leapt several feet in the air and let out a small squeak. I am not exaggerating about the distance I jumped, either. I did mention the undead lifestyle comes with a few side perks. Another was heightened senses, which told me there was only one person outside my door (I know what you're thinking; if I can hear so well, how did they catch me by surprise? Well, I don't go around using my heightened senses willy-nilly. Just think how distracting that would be, especially when I'm trying to get work done!)

Gathering my composure, I walked over to the door, undid several deadbolts, and pulled it open a few inches to see who would disturb a working vampire in the evening. As it turned out, the answer was a tall, curvy blonde in gray slacks and a red, button-down, collared shirt. The colors didn't do much to accentuate her chocolate brown eyes, but the confidence reflecting in them was all the accentuation they needed.

"Hey, Freddy," Krystal said, slipping her way past the door and giving me a hug.

"How did you know where I lived?" I asked. I was excited to see her, and should really have done a better job showing it, but at that precise moment, adrenaline was still surging strongly through me.

"We've been through this, Freddy. Mysterious agency, no name I can give out, impossible connections and information sources—you know the drill. Got any beer?" She kissed me on the cheek and meandered over to my fridge. Getting ahold of myself, I shut the door firmly and re-engaged all of my locks before turning my attention to the blonde rifling through my meagerly stocked refrigerator.

Again (as I often had since reuniting and striking up something of a romantic interlude with her after the reunion), I wondered if we were drawn together out of necessity—her living a life she couldn't tell a normal man about, and me . . . well, me being of those things she's not allowed to talk about.

"We have *got* to get you stocking some beer. Merlot, blood, and brie. That's all that's in here. You're killing me, Freddy." She shut the fridge door and gave me one of her careless smiles. Whatever her lifestyle had done to her over the past ten years, it had certainly made her beautiful. Dare I hope this wasn't just about convenience?

"Well, I would have prepared if I had known you were coming by. I haven't seen you since our date after the reunion fiasco," I said.

"Ugh, I know. Sorry about that. Had to fly to Greece to track down some marauding ghouls. Took forever, and the company plan doesn't cover unauthorized international calls to undead romantic interests," she said, waltzing over to my couch and plopping down.

"Ah yes, well . . . they, um . . . they don't actually know we went out, do they? I mean, I imagine they would be less than chipper to learn that one of their agents is dating a vampire," I said, sitting down in the chair catty-corner to the couch.

"Of course they know. I reported it before we even went out. No cares about that though. They just wouldn't pony up to pay the long distance charges," she said.

"They don't care that you're dating a vampire?" I don't think I did a very good job keeping the shock out of my voice.

"Nope, that would be discriminatory. We work hard to maintain good relationships with all parahuman communities, and that includes Undead Americans," she explained.

"You must be making this up."

"Totally serious. There are equal rights laws, a voting system, even tax benefits to hiring Undead Americans if you run a business. It's a big, wide world, Freddy. You should really leave your little bat cave sometime and go see it. You'd be surprised at some of the things out there," Krystal said, getting up from the couch and coming over to my chair. She set herself gently on my lap. "For example, you could come out with me tonight. We could go to a greasy diner, pick up some decent beer, maybe even take in a midnight showing at a movie theatre and not pay attention to what's on the screen."

"I, uh . . . um . . . yes . . . well . . . " Being a vampire grants you many things. A sudden burst of intuition and confidence with the opposite sex sitting directly on top of you is sadly not one of them.

Krystal laughed. "Glad to see you still get flustered so easily. It was always one of your more adorable traits. So, you want to come?"

"Well . . . ahem . . . I suppose I have almost caught up on tonight's work."

"Great!" Krystal hopped from my lap and pulled me up with her. "It'll be tons of fun. Just you, and me, and the city at night." She began unlocking my door and pulling it open. "There's just one little thing I have to stop and do while we're out. Quick errand, won't take a minute." With that, she unlatched the final lock and all but bounced out the door.

"What kind of errand?" I asked as I hurried to catch up, stopping outside to re-lock all the bolts. She paid no attention to me though, galloping down the hallway and out into the parking lot.

"Krystal?" I called as I finished locking and moved briskly down the hall to follow her. "I'm serious. Where are we going? What kind of errand?"

2.

"WELCOME, EVERYONE, AND THANK YOU for coming to this week's Black Banshee Role Playing Game." The speaker was young, maybe sixteen or seventeen, wearing what had to be a suit from the 1950s and sporting glasses and a haircut that matched. He moved with a strange confidence; then again, perhaps it was only strange because it was confidence of any kind, and in this setting.

Scattered around me were a variety of people, ranging in age from the frequent teenager to the more elusive adult. Most were wearing somewhat elaborate costumes. Many of them sported fake fangs and were wearing makeup in order to pale their skin, a few wore heavily furred gloves and wolf masks, and there was even one person who looked to have stolen his ghost-sheet costume straight out of Charlie Brown.

"As all of you should know, my name is Neil, and I will be your Game Master this evening. Now, since all of you registered your characters beforehand, my assistant—Albert, over there— will be working the table near the front. We do ask that you check in, take your badge, and keep it somewhere visible all night long. Your badge identifies your character name, race, and what faction, if any, you belong to. I'll remind those of you who are new to our LARP that any information in black is considered general knowledge, and information in red is known only to those of you in the same race. Gaining the red information will have to happen through interaction, so please, no metagaming. Albert will also hand you our general rules sheet, so check in as soon as possible. Once everyone is accounted for, we can get this game started!" He threw his fist in the air at that last line, and then took a deep bow. He left his soapbox of a stage (yes, it was actually a soapbox; no, I have no idea where he found such a thing) to the sound of scattered clapping. (If you're wondering, I was most certainly not one of those clapping.)

"Please explain to me how this is an errand," I asked Krystal, with as much unfriendliness as I was able to conjure. Which is to say, not much.

"It's no big deal," she said, taking my hand and leading me over to a line that had formed around a large folding table decorated with badges, sheets of a paper, and one solo attendant (presumably Albert) doing his damndest to keep up with the influx of people swarming him. "There have been some reports of a shambling figure seen here after hours, and a few reports of missing animals. Ten bucks says it's just some kid staying late to practice his act and a coincidental upturn in runaways, but I have to come check it out anyway."

"Well . . . how long does it usually last?" I asked, already feeling the familiar symptoms of caving in to whatever what someone else wanted me to do.

"Only three hours, and we should be gone in half that," Krystal said. She wrapped her arms around me, then slithered her hand up to my head and gently raked her fingernails through my hair as she pressed in close, making her . . . non-mental assets very apparent. "I promise there will still be ample time to go ignore a movie," she purred.

Something that doesn't entirely suck about being a vampire, pun unremorsefully intended, is the ability to sense and pick up on things humans miss all the time. For example, when Krystal wrapped herself around me like that, I heard her heartbeat increase, felt the warmth of blood flow to various places, and smelled the increase of pheromones she put out. It's one thing to have a beautiful woman blatantly flirting with you; it's a whole other thing to have biological evidence she really means it.

"Um . . . well . . . we . . . okay," I said, giving in, to exactly no one's surprise (especially not my own). Krystal kissed me on the cheek and pulled back while dialing down the sex appeal, though not quite letting either slip away from me entirely.

"You're the best, Freddy. And who knows? You might even have fun."

"I seriously doubt that," I said as we moved ever so slowly through the throng of would-be players clamoring for their badges.

"Why not?" Krystal asked.

"I can't do pretend very well. I mean, I like the idea of acting, but I get so nervous. Remember when I tried out for the theatre program sophomore year? I vomited all over the stage before I even finished my first line."

"Oh yeah! You know, I'd forgotten that," she said. "Still, it wasn't as bad as when you tried out for choir."

"Let us not re-visit that rest stop on memory road. My stomach is churning already," I said.

Krystal let out a surprisingly throaty laugh. It drew looks from the few un-distracted players around us. I suppose they were sensitive to the idea of laughter, but upon seeing it wasn't directed at them, most turned their attention back to the table. There were a few who didn't, though, and given how Krystal looked in comparison to most of the others there, I could hardly blame them.

"You can't throw up, dum-dum," Krystal told me when she was done giggling. "I mean that literally. Your kind doesn't have the ability to do that."

"We don't?" I asked.

"Have you tried?"

"Why on earth would I try?" I said, a touch exasperated that she still seemed to know more about what I was than I did.

"Hmm, good point. Yes, you can't puke. It's one of those things you lost."

"Oh," I said. I didn't mean for it to sound sad. It certainly wasn't a great loss, the ability to void my stomach in a backward direction, but it was yet one more thing that made me less human. And those were becoming all too frequent for my liking.

"Cheer up, buttercup," Krystal said as we reached the front of the line. "One day, I'll help you discover all the things you've gained. I think you'll be pleasantly surprised by a few of them. I know I will," she whispered to me before turning to Albert the Attendant. With that line lingering in my ear and echoing through my libido, I watched as she did an about-face to speak with the young man staring up at her (though not quite as up as he should have been in order to see her face).

"Krystal Jenkins and Freddy Fletcher checking in," she said with a warm smile. It seemed to catch poor Albert off guard, as he suddenly became flustered and began digging about for our badges. Of course, given how unfriendly everyone seemed to have been to him, I could understand why he would falter at a changeup. He was young and wore a dirty black shirt and dirtier black pants. I wasn't sure what the organizer had made him do before this, but I could only imagine it involved digging, because that kid reeked of earth. Not a bad smell really, just a potent one.

He finally found our badges and handed them both to Krystal. He hesitated for a moment before letting go and looked at mine, then up at me, then back at mine.

"Is that what you're going to wear?" Albert asked in a not-quite-squeaky, not-quite-grown-up teenage voice. Though the question was probing, his tone was surprisingly friendly.

I looked at my ensemble. I was wearing a robin's egg blue sweater vest on top of a white button-down shirt along with a pair of black slacks and sensible black shoes. I did stand out a bit compared to everyone else, but I hadn't really been told to dress for this, now had I?

"Um, is that a problem?" I asked him.

"Not a problem, just wondering. Your character is your character," he said, handing me a sheet of paper; he then motioned me to the side so he could help the next person. "Personally, I think it's really neat that you decided to take your costume in a different direction. You two have a great night."

I joined Krystal a few strides away from the line. "What's wrong with my outfit?" I asked her.

"It doesn't fit your character so well," she said, a wicked grin lighting up her face.

"Oh, yes, on that note, this whole event requires registration and character creation beforehand. So how is it that you just happened to have an ID badge ready for me and under my name?" I asked, really just for form. The answer was all too obvious.

"I thought this would suck, so I wanted company. Sexy, dangerous vampire company," she said, the laughing smile staying firmly on her face as she reached out and put her hand against my chest.

"Shhh!" I fervently whispered, welling up with panic. "What if someone hears you?"

"Check your badge there, Freddy. It's black-print information. Everyone will know when they see you," Krystal said, pulling her own badge out and affixing it to her shirt.

"Huh?" I said idiotically, and then looked at the front of my clothes. Sure enough, my badge was affixed— clearly slipped on there when she touched my chest—carefully on the breast pocket of my sweater vest. It took me a moment to unravel its words as I read them upside down.

It said:

Name: Count Fredrick
Race: Vampire

Then, below that in red print, it said:

Faction: Revivalist

"You made me a vampire?"

"You did say you hated pretending."

"Are you one too?" I asked, not bothering to read her tag. Given where she'd attached it on her shirt, there was no easy way to read it without being something of a pervert.

"I'm Sunny the Succubus," she said, her voice up a few registers and her tone lilting. She sounded like a mix between the stereotype of a cheerleader and the stereotype of a valley girl.

"What's a succubus?" I asked.

"Demon slut," she said simply, in her own voice. Ah, well then, that made the accent quite appropriate. I wondered for a moment just how much time she put into preparing for this role. But that thought process was interrupted as she took my hand once more.

"Looks like they're almost ready to start," she said, slipping back into her character tone. "Come on. Let's go mingle!"

3.

"ALL RIGHT, EVERYONE, THANK YOU ALL for checking in," Neil the Game Master said as he climbed back atop his soapbox to address us. Something about the kid still struck me as weird. It wasn't the clothing or his style either; he was odd, but nowhere near the weirdest guy in attendance. It was just something in the way he moved. I couldn't put my finger on it, but I knew it was there. I didn't really pay that much mind to it, though. I mean, after all, I was a vampire who hid the fact that he was a vampire, standing in a park pretending to be the thing that I usually pretend I'm not. Who was I to throw stones at weird?

"Before we begin, I just want to go over the rules on your sheets, so that everyone knows the system and we can all have fun. To start with, we do not do realistic battle simulations here. I saw some of you bring your foam weapons, but, unfortunately, we've had some lawsuit trouble in the past and have decided it's not worth the risk. Any fighting will be resolved by a match of rock-paper-scissors. If you fight someone of the same race, it will be a best 2-out-of-3 match to represent how much more difficult these fights are," Neil said, reading to the crowd from his sheet. I heard mumbles as a few costumed participants set down large, foam replica-weapons on the ground, faces all but dripping in disappointment. Albert scuttled around swiftly, gathering up the weapons and setting them on the folding table where the badges had been.

"Now then, aside from combat, all of you have your own powers and abilities. These are written on the backs of your badges should you forget or need to prove to another player this is a power you really possess. Success is considered automatic, unless another player has immunity to that particular ability. In cases where a player with a power deals with another player who only has a resistance to that power—not an immunity—we will again be going to the rock-paper-scissors method of resolving who comes out on top," Neil continued. If that made no sense to you, don't feel bad. I was slack-jawed and flummoxed by the time he finished that part. I simply hoped I would either figure it out as I played or be gone soon enough that it wouldn't matter.

"Last, but certainly not least, this is a Live Action Role Playing game. All of you have gathered here as the new emperor of the city requested, to try and forge an alliance between the various supernatural cultures living in his domain. For this to be the most enjoyable event it can be, I ask that you truly commit to your roles. Do not break character unless it is a vital emergency. In this way, we can forget the names we have behind our badges and truly immerse ourselves in tonight's identities." I had to admit, I was a touch envious; this kid was a better public speaker than I had ever been. I'd tried to correct that particular failing on many occasions—each an unmitigated disaster—and often with gastrointestinal consequences. "And now, I'll ask you to meet up with those of your race and faction as you arrive at the emperor's ball. When I step down from here, the game has begun, and I am your ruler: Emperor Nikolai."

He didn't step down as much as hop, but the symbolism was there, and we got the message. I turned to ask Krystal what I should do now, only to find her gone. I whipped my head around looking for her, but before I could do more than glance to my side, a small hand grabbed me by the shoulder.

It belonged to a proportionally small woman, maybe early twenties in age, wearing heavy white makeup and a long black trench coat coupled with a corset and leather pants. Her badge told me her character name was Maria, and that she was a vampire like me. The fake fangs I saw when she spoke a moment later assured me that she was definitely a vampire only while this game was in progress.

"Good evening, Count Fredrick. Our Lord Drake will be so pleased another nightwalker loyal to the cause has joined us this evening," she said, slurring slightly due to the fangs.

"Um . . . yay, and verily I hath come?"

The look she gave me said quite clearly that my vampire impression had missed the mark. Luckily for me, the girl was a pro; she rolled with it well. "There is no need to imitate the high language, Count Fredrick. Clearly you were turned recently, so this generation's tongue is your own. Speak freely and comfortably, for our Lord Drake cares nothing of cultural differences, only of loyalty and dedication. We are all equally united under our cause."

"Okay . . . thanks. And, you know, just so I know we're on the same page here, which 'cause' are you talking about? I'm active in a few of them actually. I used to do walks for cancer before the whole turning thing and—"

Mercifully, Maria cut me off with a finger against my lips and one pointing to the red writing on my badge that said "Revivalist." I finally noticed she had the same writing on her own. The pieces fell into place. Well, admittedly, they were more jammed into place by force, but I got the point, and that was what mattered.

"Oh, yes, right! The *true* cause. Forgive me, I have not eaten anyone in a few days, and I've grown a bit muddled round the temples, if you know what I mean," I said, thinking on my feet. I really did get foggy when I went a few days without blood, so hopefully that was a part of this vampire mythos as well.

"Of course, good Count. With the preparations for tonight's event, all of us have been exceptionally busy. I can hardly fault you for putting the cause's success over the needs of your own thirst. Worry not, for tonight enough blood shall flow to sate the hunger in all of our throats. But come . . . we must hurry to meet with Lord Drake. Time is already short, and even the lesser monsters have ears with which to hear," Maria said, tugging me toward a big cluster of trees.

We went through that cluster, then through a few more, down a twisting dirt road, and then through more trees. I was making a mental note to myself to take a free night and see just how big this freaking park was when we finally broke into a clearing. It would have seemed like a natural clearing in a real forest, save for the dozen figures in makeup and the picnic table located in the center.

"Ah, my maiden Maria returns to us from her mission seeking stragglers," said a large man wearing a velvet ruffled-shirt, a leather cape, and what looked like combat boots.

"Aye, my Lord Drake, I come bearing Count Fredrick. His invitation to meet us separately from the others of our ilk was lost, so I escorted him to join us tonight," Maria said, using her jacket to do a curtsey as she spoke. I had to give the girl credit; she was good at this. She knew I had no idea what was going on and had still managed to weave me into the story quite nicely.

"Arise, my servant," said the large man I could only surmise was Lord Drake. "We have much to do this eve, and so precious little time to do it." Lord Drake turned to me. "And you, good Count, we thank you for your support. As you can see, our force is small, so we shall seek victory through strategy and cunning. A single loyal vampire may very well be the difference between success and failure."

Lord Drake walked over to the picnic table and settled down his considerable heft. The other "vampires" followed suit, so I made my way over as well. I had no idea what Krystal was up to, but it seemed like my best bet was to play along and blend in until she finished her job and we could bail.

"My dark children," Lord Drake began. "For too long we have been forced to live this way. Feeding in secret, locked within the shadows, existing as nothing more than myth and fancy in the eyes of the cattle we call humans." There were mumbles of agreement that rippled through the table. I myself made mumbles of non-committal curiosity. The differences are subtle, but very important.

"We have suffered much humiliation at the hands of those in charge. Worse yet, most of our kind have been domesticated. They truly believe a vampire is meant to slink and sip, instead of dominate and destroy. We are the strongest beasts here, and yet we walk as if dogs with tails between our legs, ashamed of our own power and grandeur." The agreement was getting a touch more boisterous now. I was oddly reminded of pep rallies in high school. Everyone was getting fired up around me, yet it was abundantly clear that I was not a part of what was going on.

"And now, the final insult: A mere human trickster, a mage, being made the emperor of our sweet city. This is a blow which I fear we cannot bear. I will not bow to cattle. I will not scrape my knee to the ground for nothing more than a human with a few cantrips. That is why we gather here tonight, my dark children, so that we may carry out our plan to revive our rightful place in this world's hierarchy."

They weren't mumbling anymore; they were downright cheering. The only ones who were still moderately subdued were me and my guide, Maria, who stared on with wonder and fascination in her eyes.

“Tonight, we do what should have been done long ago. Tonight, we remind this world that vampires are creatures to be feared, not handled. Tonight, we leave the shadows and put ourselves back on the path to our rightful place as rulers over the cattle and the lesser monsters.” Lord Drake leaned in close and the cheering died in an instant. Everyone was still as death, no pun intended, as the great Lord Drake licked his lips and let his next words fly.

“Tonight, my dark children, we kill the emperor!”

4.

"I HAVE GOT TO STOP LEAVING THE apartment," I mumbled to myself as we skulked through the forest toward the main area where everyone was assembled. And I do mean "skulked" in a very literal way. It seems all of the Revivalist vampires had an ability to blend in with the scenery and become more or less invisible. According to the back of the badge, the way we signified this was by moving hunched over and carefully, with our index fingers on both sides of our heads.

That's right. I was hunching my way through the forest with finger horns.

Somehow, when I was human and dreamed about a different kind of life, one where I was powerful and immortal, this was a scenario I had never imagined. True, most of those fantasies had been cheap rip-offs of well-done films, involving a socially gregarious, unstoppably cool version of me. I couldn't even fathom why someone would incorporate something as asinine as finger horns into their own fantasy. Still, I was supposed to blend, so blend I did.

It took us considerable time to get back to the main event, mostly because of our slow-moving pace, but finally we parted a section of trees and found ourselves faced with the mingling crowd and a folding table stocked with foam weapons. Lord Drake jerked his head northward, and we began our agonizing walk in that direction.

Let me tell you something: I've been forced to do some ridiculous things in my lifetime. I've put my head in the toilet for swirlies, eaten dirt, even been made to dance like a cha-cha girl, all to avoid being beaten up. For the dickens though, I cannot imagine what would make someone willingly do what we did as we crept through the crowd. We did our hunch walk with our finger horns, skulking through them, all the while pretending they couldn't see us. Adding to the oddness, they all clearly noticed us and wanted to know what was going on, but had to pretend we were invisible.

It was like embarrassment and stupidity, compacted. To their credit, not one person broke character and approached us, and we moved past the majority of the players into a more open area on the north side of the park. From there, we could see Emperor Nikolai speaking in hushed tones to some of the other players. One of them was the person with the Charlie Brown ghost costume, and one looked to be wearing a werewolf mask, so they were pretty obvious. The other two I recognized even more easily, though. They were Albert the Henchman and my own dear Sunny the Succubus.

I briefly wondered why she was a part of the little pow-wow, but I guessed it made sense. If you need to investigate, why not go right to the top?

None of that changed the plan, though. Lord Drake had known that Emperor Nikolai would be speaking to a few delegates at a time, with only his servant Albert as protection. I wasn't sure what kind of monster Albert was, and I hadn't had a chance to ask, but Lord Drake seemed pretty certain we would be able to overpower him easily. The goal here was for us to creep up on the separated few and spring into action. Each of us was supposed to do battle with one of the delegates, while Lord Drake and two of his servants took down the emperor. That way the "kill" would be assigned to Lord Drake and he would then have cause to lobby that he should be the new emperor. New emperor meant he'd make the rules, which meant no more hiding from the humans, and yada yada yada.

The main point I had gleaned from all of that was that I needed to pick a person and play rock-paper-scissors with them. Either they won, or I did. After that, none of this was my problem anymore, and hopefully Krystal would be ready to go.

We resumed our skulking, moving delicately, yet purposefully, toward our soon-to-be-deposed emperor. Lord Drake, Maria, and another girl broke off to circle around toward the rear, where the emperor was located. The rest of us continued creeping up on our targets. Since I was near her side anyway, I locked my vision on Krystal and decided to "battle" her. I think it was because I was focused only on her that I noticed the quick gesture she made, scratching the top of her nose with her thumb. I had only an instant to ponder why she would use a thumb instead of a finger before strange words rang through the air.

"*Ectorim Novendum, Bicradalio.*" It was Neil's voice, and it rang out with authority and power, more than I would have ever thought the kid capable of, despite his earlier public speaking proficiency. When he spoke again, though, it was somewhat less impressive.

"As you have all noticed, you are now frozen in place thanks to my spell," Emperor Nikolai said, closing the large black tome he had obviously read from and handing it to Albert. “None of you have applicable immunities or resistances, and yes, we are quite aware that you Revivalists are here. Your camouflage power was dispelled the moment I froze you.”

There was a ripple of gasping shock from our vampires as well as nearby players.

“I’d suspected for some time that you might try an uprising, so I took necessary precautions,” he continued. At this point Krystal, or I should say *Sunny*, bounced over and stood smiling dumbly as he slipped an arm around her. “My new consort here is a succubus, and as most of you should know, they possess the ability to see past all veils and illusions.”

Emperor Nikolai released his grip on Sunny and walked over to Lord Drake—who, to his credit, was remaining stock still—and then leaned into Drake’s face. “So, the great Lord Drake is reduced to nothing more than a mere mannequin. How elegantly pathetic. You underestimated me, Drake; you thought that just because I was genetically a human, I would go down easy. After all, what possible threat can a mere mage be?” Emperor Nikolai stepped back from Drake and returned to his own group, taking the black book from Albert’s waiting hands.

“You should have done a little research first, Drake. You might have realized I’m not just a mage. I’m a necromancer, a spell caster with power over all forms of death, and that includes the undead. Binding your walking corpses required little more effort from me than turning a page." Emperor Nikolai gave Drake a look of sheer condescension, gloating without restraint. "Now, the only question is what to do with you all. I think I shall unbind you, after wrapping you in silver chains of course, so that Albert may escort you back into the forest. I will finish up my party with my dear subjects, and spend the time thinking of a fitting punishment for you."

With that, the emperor clapped his hands and Albert pulled a large chest from behind a tree. In it were long lengths of chain, as well as several padlocks. Albert started with Lord Drake, then slowly made his way to each of us, covering us in the chains so we could barely move, and then connecting us into one giant undead chain gang.

None of which was my biggest concern. You see, my problem had started the minute good old Neil shouted those gibberish words. I was frozen like ice, unable to move even my own eyes. That spell of his had been real, and I was captured by it, which meant three things:

1. I wasn't the only *real* monster here.
2. I was the worst possible race to try and stop him.
3. We were in deep shit. *Again.*

5.

WALKING BACK INTO THE FOREST WAS something of a chore. Neil had used another spell to unfreeze us, and it had given me back my range of motion, but there was still the fact that we were all shackled together, and that made the commute pretty challenging. In addition, Albert had been oddly thorough in chaining our hands behind our backs and our legs close together.

Everyone else seemed to be pretty into the scene, impressed that Neil had planned this far ahead and gone to such lengths for realism. I was the only one truly concerned, but that was because I was the only one who knew Neil had used a set of real spells and had bound us with real chains, though thankfully not real silver ones. Silver doesn't hurt me, per se, but it does weaken me and, if exposed to my skin, makes me break out in a terrible rash. Even with undead regeneration, it takes days to fade. Seriously, ten buckets of calamine won't soothe the itch that gleaming metal leaves behind.

Albert was moving up and down the line, giving direction to the front while coordinating our movements in the back. Officially, he was there to make sure none of us tried to escape. I think in truth he was just making sure we didn't go tumbling down like a row of dominoes. I watched him as he moved, watched him more carefully than I had the rest of that evening. He was quick with his movements, not quite fluid, but well above jerky. He was about as pale as the rest of the made-up vampire squad, but a few shades above my own dead skin. And he still reeked of earth. The kid must have either been playing in the mud every time we didn't see him or had spent a few days marinating in dirt.

I'm sure a few of you have gotten there already, but this was the point where it all finally sank home. Constantly obedient, reeked of earth, dirty clothes, and paler than normal skin; it was clear Albert wasn't alive. I focused my hearing, first noticing the sounds of the forest, then the mingling partygoers to my rear, and then at last

I heard the heartbeats of those around me. My senses seemed to hone in on that, like they'd been looking for it all along. I shook off the implications of what that probably meant and began listening to one person at a time. Once I was confident I had heard a beat from every one of my captured cohorts, I turned my focus to Albert.

I got nothing. Not a heartbeat, nor a gasp for air—nothing but the sounds of his bones scraping, his muscles twanging as he scampered about. Hey, I said vampire senses were powerful, not that they weren't gross.

All of this sounds like it happened quickly, but the truth is that we had finally reached our destination by the time I confirmed my hypothesis (I had to split my focus between listening and walking, after all). He moved down the line, wearing a giant smile as he helped each of us sit down, so we would be comfortable while we waited for the emperor to come judge us. I was at the end of the line, so I was left standing 'til the end.

By providence or coincidence, I had been further away from most of the others when we were frozen, which meant I had a fair amount of chain separating me from the player in front of me. I began carefully inching my way backward. When Albert sat me down, I wanted as much space from anyone else as possible. I had some questions that were most definitely not for public hearing.

It took some time due to Albert's care with helping each player, but he finally reached me. He stood behind my back and told me to slowly lower my knees. I did as instructed, waiting until my butt was on the ground and he was bent over my shoulders—just about to let go of me—before speaking.

"So," I said, trying with all my might to be casual. "What are you anyway, Albert?"

Instead of answering, he released his grip and walked around in front of me. He then took a knee so we were eye to eye and pointed to his badge. There, in clear black ink, it said: "Zombie."

"Are you really?" I asked, with what I hoped was an arched eyebrow.

"Of course. I am Albert the Unstoppable Zombie, raised by Emperor Nikolai and existing only to serve his every whim," Albert declared proudly.

"No . . . dammit, you're not getting the point. Forget the game. Are you an actual zombie?" I asked again.

Albert's relentlessly cheerful face grew wary and worried. Even I could tell I was at least on the right track. "Don't be silly," he said, hushing his tone slightly. "There's no such thing as zombies."

"Right. Just like there's no such thing as necromancers who cast real spells and take a bunch of real chained up people out into the woods with no witnesses."

Albert didn't say anything after that, just widened his eyes and began chewing on his lower lip.

"Okay, I'll be honest with you," I said. "I know you're a real zombie, and Neil is a real necromancer. I don't really care about either of those things. Live and let live; that's my philosophy. Just tell me that all of this is part of the game, that there is nothing sinister afoot, and I'll hang out and play along until my date comes to pick me up for the movie. I really don't want trouble; I just wanted to go to the movies. So just say it's part of the game. *Please.*"

Albert stopped chewing and looked at me with an expression that was very much like a puppy that slipped up and peed on the rug—guilty and apologetic, with the resignation that he couldn't change what had already happened.

"Fudge," I swore.

"I'm really, really sorry," Albert said, rocking back off his knee and sitting next to me Indian style. "I wanted to warn you guys, or stop him, but I just couldn't."

"Because you're a supernatural being under his thrall?" I asked.

"No, because he's my best friend. My only friend, actually. Even when I was alive, it was the just the two of us. He'd come up with crazy schemes, and I'd follow along. He just got so wrapped up in things. I could never seem to talk him out of stuff. Besides, most of the time I just felt lucky to have even one friend. I mean, there was never all that much interesting about me, and now that I'm dead, I'm even less socially desirable."

"Yeah, I know how that goes," I said, summoning the most consoling tone I could under the circumstances. Okay, sure he had been part of a scheme to kidnap a bunch of people for heaven only knew what, but I couldn't help feeling for the kid. I'd been in about the same boat my whole life, and most of my afterlife. "I wasn't exactly Mr. Popular myself."

"Few people who come to these events are. That's why they were so much fun. I don't imagine you've had it quite that bad, though. I saw the girl you came here with. And besides, at least you're not some undead freak," Albert said. It was weird. Even when trying to mope, his voice still had a happy, sing-songy style.

"Um . . . well . . . that's not entirely true," I said.

Albert looked up from the ground he had been staring at and directly at me. It was less like he was looking at me, though, and more like he was studying me carefully. "Just how untrue is it?" Albert asked.

In response, I opened my mouth and showed him my human-looking teeth. With a bit of concentration, I did the trick I was finally getting the hang of—letting my canines extend to long, razor-sharp points. I then pulled them back to normal, which was much harder than letting them grow, and closed my mouth.

Albert's mouth, however, hung open in surprise. After a few minutes of opening and closing his jaw, he finally got his tongue back in working order and said, "I guess that explains how you knew Neil was the real deal."

"Unfortunately, yes it does. Wait, you're undead. Why didn't it work on you?"

Albert shrugged. "I think creatures you animate are immune from your own generic spells. You have to target them directly, or some such protocol. Neil explained it to me once after he brought me back, but I've never been smart enough to understand stuff like that."

"Oh," I said. We lapsed into silence after that, captor and captive deciding where to go from here. I opted to try and ask the question I'd never been able to ask anyone since my transformation. I mean, when was I going to get another chance like this?

"So, if it isn't prying," I said carefully. "Can I ask how you died?"

There was only silence at first, but then I heard Albert's voice say softly, "I'd rather not talk about it."

"I understand," I said quickly. "I can barely even remember my death. It seems like I've almost totally blocked it out. If you do remember yours, then I can only guess at how traumatic it must have been. I'm sorry I asked. It's just . . . you're the first undead person I've met."

"Ummmm, it isn't that it was really traumatic. Just embarrassing," Albert said.

"What makes it so bad?" I asked.

"How much do you know about autoerotic asphyxiation and the accidents that come with it?"

"You know what, I think I've got the picture," I said, words so hurried I nearly broke into a stutter. "So . . . that happened, then Neil brought you back. Was he always a necromancer?"

"Nah," Albert said quickly, obviously grateful to be off the topic of his death. "He was a science geek for years. He used to make fun of me for loving the occult and stuff like this. But after I died, apparently he went off the deep end a little bit. He even went to his grandpa for help." Albert gave his head a small shake, sending strands of his long, moderately unkempt hair in front of his dark eyes.

"Was his grandfather a necromancer too?" I asked, getting drawn in a bit.

"Not that we know of, but his grandmother was a real famous medium back in the day. Before she died, she accumulated a bunch of supposedly magical stuff, and one of the things there was that black book."

"Gotcha. So he found the book, gave it a try, and, low and behold, it's the real deal," I said, finishing the story in my mind.

"More or less. Apparently, you also have to have the talent in order for the magic to work, which Neil does; he tried a few times before he brought me back. But yeah, one day my eyes popped open, and I was underground. Crawled my way out, and there's my best friend, cackling like a mental patient and saying he's uncovered the magic of the gods."

"Sounds like your friend went on a power trip," I said carefully.

"I know. He's gotten more and more obsessed with it too. He keeps saying he needs greater power, needs to expand his abilities, needs to steal people's life force—" Albert shut his mouth quickly, but unfortunately, not even zombies can clam up fast enough to steal their own words back.

"Ah, so that's what this is about. Let me guess . . . ancient rite, kills us all, then uses our souls, or life force, or whatever to gather tremendous power for himself?" I asked, already knowing the answer.

Albert was clearly impressed. "Are you a necromancer too?"

"No." I sighed. "I'm just a numbers guy, and that means I can see an obvious pattern when it's set in front of me. Look, Albert, you seem like a good guy. We need to get out of here, and you're the one with the keys. You know what your friend is doing is wrong, so hurry and help us before—"

"Good evening, my rebellious subjects!" Neil said as he stepped into the clearing, large black tome in hand. "I trust you have all had time to contemplate your crimes and are ready for penance?"

"—that happens."

6.

"ALBERT!" I HISSED QUICKLY AS HE SCURRIED to a standing position and Neil began touring through our little makeshift captive camp. "Albert, there's still time. Don't let him do this!"

Unfortunately, I was wasting my . . . well, okay, I don't have real breath, so let's say "words." Albert was back in full submission mode. He all but scampered over to Neil, making the report that we were all here and thoroughly subjugated. The other players confirmed this, bewailing their fates at having put their trust in

Lord Drake instead of the clear superiority of Emperor Nikolai. The only exceptions to this were Lord Drake himself, Maria, and me. Lord Drake and Maria out of some sense of fictional, generic vampire pride, and me because I knew kissing ass was going to be a pointless gesture. Otherwise, I would have puckered up with the best of them.

Neil held up a hand and everyone fell silent. "My poor, misguided subjects, your Emperor has had time to cool his head and give thought to what you've done. While I am hurt that you would try to tear me from my throne, I am also complimented that a faction as powerful as your own would consider me a threat. Therefore, I am going to give you all a second chance."

There was a murmur of happiness that ran through the crowd. It seems some of my fellow captives had been sincerely concerned he would kill off their characters. The irony was palpable.

"Now, my dear assistant Albert will help you all to form a circle around me. I am doing this so that I might hold a binding ceremony. I will be letting you all live, but your powers will be sealed until the next new moon. By then, I hope we can be on better terms than we are now, and you will use your gifts to aid my kingdom instead of work against it," Neil said as he opened his book and began flipping through it.

Albert was off like a flash, starting at the front and arranging us in a chained circle around Neil. It took relatively little time, since Albert was less helping and more just picking up and moving. There were some confused faces when the scrawny kid picked up large men like they weighed nothing, but, after all, it was a night of magic and characters, so they let it slide.

Once again, I was last. As soon as Albert plucked me up, though, he whispered in my ear. "Listen, don't worry, okay? Nothing bad will happen to you. Neil is out to steal life forces, and we dead guys don't have that. Just sit through the ceremony and you'll be fine."

"And everyone else?" I whispered out the side of my mouth.

"You'll be fine," Albert repeated a moment later, quickening his step and setting me down, thus finishing the circle of chained vampires.

It was a fairly wide circle, with plenty of room between each of us. I suppose Neil had wanted some room to work, but I wondered how he would keep us in place once he started his spell, if anyone decided to move about. My question was answered quickly as I saw Albert moving from person to person, wrapping their chains around a tent stake, and then driving it into the earth on each side. It took a few moments, even with his strength, but when he finished everyone but me would have found it impossible to put up even a half-hearted struggle.

The chains and stakes weren't any sort of problem for me, though. No, I was even easier to stop. All Neil needed was three simple words, and I'd be exposed and powerless. I probably couldn't even run away before he'd snap off his magical phrase and pin my ass down. Which meant my only options were to sit through the ceremony like Albert said, or wait until Neil was distracted and try to rush him. The thought of trying to fight someone, even a small geek like Neil, made my stomach turn a bit. At least I knew I couldn't throw up, thanks to Krystal.

For a moment, I thought my mind was playing tricks on me. No sooner had I thought of Krystal than I saw her walking into the clearing. A moment later, I noticed Charlie-Brown-Ghost guy, and finally the man in the werewolf mask. Now I was really confused.

"Well, my good players, I think it is time for me to break character and let you know what is really going on," Neil said. "I'm afraid I lied earlier. None of you will be leaving this circle alive."

"We are already the proud and powerful dead!" Lord Drake shouted from his spot in the circle. I could see Maria nodding her head violently in agreement, and the rest of the vampire characters joined in with some show of support.

"You are *not*!" Neil thundered from the center of his circle. "You are sad people living a sad life playing a sad game to escape the misery of reality. The only person in this forest with any real power is myself. Behold, I've expanded my spell library and learned to take over the minds of the living." Neil held his hands and indicated the three people behind him. "These three each came to me as individuals with thoughts and dreams. Tonight, I turned them into nothing more than puppets for my enjoyment."

I really wasn't comfortable with the way his eyes lingered on Krystal when he said "enjoyment." I tried taking some deep breaths out of habit to calm my stomach. It was looking more and more like our only chance of getting out of here would be if I could rush him fast enough. Behind my back, I gently snapped through a few links of chain.

"I am a god among men, and you are nothing but painted-up children playing pretend," Neil continued, sneering as he talked, no longer able to hide his sense of superiority. The players were beginning to get a little antsy. He had broken character a long time ago, yet he still seemed intent on doing them harm. A few even tested their bonds, realizing for the first time just how helpless they had really become.

"Tonight, however, your pitiful lives will have meaning," Neil said as he began flipping through his book once more. "Tonight, your souls, your life essence, will be used as a catalyst to fuel my own power. As your life flows into me, it will gain the purpose it's lacked all these years with all of you. It is a beautiful trade, don't you agree? You trade your lives, and in exchange, you gain the fulfillment of having helped this city's next ruler rise to his position."

The players were panicking now; you'd have had to be an idiot not to see how drunk on his own magic Neil had become. Some were flexing violently against their chains. Others seemed to be crying and giving in to whatever this mad child had planned for them. I kept my eyes trained on Neil and worked my way through the chains, bit by bit. I probably wouldn't have a chance until he began reading his spell.

"But enough chatter. I'm anxious to begin my life as a super being, and I'm sure you are all anxious to help. Minions!" Neil called. The three behind him stood at attention. "You will surround me now. Should anyone break free somehow, your job will be to restrain them until I am able to finish my spell. Let nothing disturb your exalted master!"

The three followed his orders instantly, forming a tight triangle around him so that no angle of entry would go unseen. They stared out at us, revolving slowly to keep fresh eyes on each prisoner as they turned. No one would get bored; no one would let something slip. Credit where it was due; I had to admit Neil hadn't fallen into the villain trope of overconfidence, even if he had monologued his evil plan.

"Well, this just sucks," I muttered, still breaking through the chains, but with less enthusiasm. I'd had enough trouble getting my mind around the idea of trying to charge Neil head on. I didn't know how I was going to get through an innocent puppet without hurting them, especially if that puppet happened to be my date. I watched her as she moved: smooth, definite, without hesitation. In that moment, I could clearly see how she was an agent that dealt with supernatural beings. The girl had physical training, which only served to make my job harder.

"Ah, here it is," Neil said, stopping his turning and lighting up his face with a terrifying smile. "Goodbye, mortality. *Oncidentum, rapishadum*, GHAAAA!"

For the record, that last line wasn't part of the spell. The moment he had begun chanting, I snapped through the remainder of my chains and sprang to my feet as fast as my vampire abilities would allow. As it turned out, though, even a hopped up vampire takes longer to stand than it takes for a trained agent to withdraw and utilize a Taser. Into his crotch. And hold it there.

"Three things, shithead," Krystal said as she released the Taser and Neil fell to the ground. "First off, you are under arrest for use of necromancy magic without a license. Secondly, never monologue. It gives away your intentions and gives everyone else time to prepare. And lastly, magic is fantastic, but it's no match for my wand of brain shocking." With that, she knelt down and gave him one last blast to the chest. Neil was out, and I mean "out" as in "drooling and twitching" out. The other two puppets, unfortunately, seemed to be carrying out orders still. They rushed at Krystal, attacking the woman who had broken their master's commandment.

She whipped around quickly, tripping the werewolf with her leg and slamming it with her Taser as it tried to get up. The werewolf dropped like a hammer and Krystal turned quickly, expecting the ghost to be attacking her other side. What she found instead, though, was me holding the ghost horizontally by its hips over my head.

"I thought you might need a hand," I said, in what I hoped was a lighthearted manner.

"My hero," Krystal replied with a grin. She ambled over, pulled off the ghost's sheet, and put the Taser into the arm of the young woman who had been beneath it. The struggling over my head ceased, and I gently set the girl down, rolling up her costume and putting it under her head as a pillow.

This all sounds like a peaceful ballet of coordinated movements, but it was amid the screaming, shock, and crying of the other vampire prisoners. All of it topped off by a wail from Albert, as he rushed forward and cradled Neil's head.

"You killed him! You killed my friend!" Albert moaned.

"Did not," Krystal said, ignoring the calls of the prisoners surrounding her and walking back over to the unconscious mage and the grieving zombie. "Anyone who can use magic has a slight resistance to all forms of energy. That includes electricity. It required three bursts to take him down just like it would a normal person. He's fine, or at least he will be when he wakes up."

"But he's under arrest," Albert said, worry thick in his voice. "Won't he be killed once he gets charged with what he tried to do tonight?"

"Don't be an idiot," Krystal said. "Ceremonies aren't illegal. I'm only charging him with magic usage without a license. You have to be trained and certified to do magic out in the open like this."

"Oh," Albert said, relief washing over his face.

"Truth be told, you should be worried more about yourself than your friend," Krystal said, as she knelt down and picked up Neil's book. "Zombies are only allowed to exist on work visas."

"What does that mean?" Albert asked.

"Zombies need a job, or they lose focus and create havoc. Your buddy here is unlicensed, so he can't offer you employment. And it's almost impossible for zombies to get work, other than with the necromancer that created them, so we usually have to terminate them," Krystal explained.

"And, when you say 'terminate' . . ." Albert let the sentence trail off.

"'Return you to your place in the natural world' is the way the higher ups put it," she said, finishing his thought.

"Oh no," Albert said, shaking slightly despite the lack of any biological need to.

It was a heartbreaking night for the poor kid. He thought his only friend was dead, discovered he needed a job he wouldn't be able to get, and found out he would likely wind up dead again. My empathy went out to the now not-as-upbeat zombie. He obviously had some self-worth issues, and he definitely needed to stand up for himself more, but it seemed like he really had a good heart. And that was a set of circumstances I found all too easy to empathize with.

"Hold on, Krystal," I said, butting into the conversation. "Exactly what kind of tax benefits come from employing Undead Americans?"

7.

"THIS MOVIE IS GOD-AWFUL," I SAID, taking a handful of popcorn and crunching down.

"Mmhmm. That's why I picked it. I knew no one else would be here," Krystal said, gesturing to the empty theatre.

"That couldn't have anything to do with the fact that it's three in the morning. Or that this theatre doesn't even do late-night showings."

"Hey, I promised you a movie, so I called in a favor."

"Uh huh. One day, we need to have a talk about you and your job and your favors," I said, with a mustering of authority.

"Did you want to do that tonight?" Krystal said, her eyes growing serious. There was a hardness there that worried me a bit. I might be the more powerful between the two of us, but I didn't really think I was the stronger.

"Well . . . no, not tonight. I think we've had enough of your job for this evening," I said, as I verbally scampered away from that previous authoritative tone.

"Oh, like it was all bad. You got a new assistant and roommate out of the deal," Krystal said, her eyes softening and her usual smile dancing into place.

"I couldn't let the kid just be put back in the ground. Besides, I really do need the help. Still, I guess now I'll have to buy blood *and* animal corpses to keep us both fed," I said.

"Zombies don't eat flesh, Freddy," Krystal corrected. "They don't eat anything, not for nutrition. That's what makes them perfect servants. They don't need to eat, drink, or sleep. All they do is work, and in the case of yours, file documents."

"Wait," I said. "The whole reason we went out there was because of reports of a lumbering figure late at night and an increase in missing pets. If that wasn't Albert, then who was it?"

"Neil," she said, as she turned her attention to the frankenbeast skulking on the screen. "I got a full confession out of him while you were getting Albert set up at your place. He was out practicing to try and bring Albert back. He would kill the pets, then try to revive them. The one time he succeeded, he let the damn thing wander away, which means I get to spend tomorrow hunting for a freaking zombie rabbit."

"That will be an annoyance. Won't you have to wipe the memories or something of all the vampire characters that saw Neil lose it?" I asked.

"Feh, I wish we had mind-wiping abilities. That would be sweet," Krystal said. "No, we already had the cops that came to unchain them feed them a story. Neil was just some kid who went off his meds and was going to chop them up. Luckily, they had an undercover agent there in the form of me, and I was able to subdue him before he committed any real crimes."

"What about when you said he was under arrest for magic without a license?"

"Playing to his delusion so he would come along more peacefully."

"Oh," I said. "Well, I guess that makes sense. You know, for all his faults, Neil really did seem to care about his friend, though. The whole reason he started this was to bring back his buddy."

Krystal nodded. "He's talented, and he got into it for the right reasons. He just went a little nutty. It happens to everyone without training. Part of the sentence will be enrolling him in courses with a master. In a few months, he'll be able to control the megalomania and still use magic. Kid with his talent will probably be certified in a year or so."

"Yeah, I wanted to ask you about that. If Neil is so good at magic, why didn't his mind control spell work on you?"

"Pshh, no one tells me what to do," she said with a wink.

"That seemed like a dodge," I said.

"Very good, fang boy." Krystal lifted up the armrest that separated our two seats. "Now, do you want to chase this topic and keep talking," she said as she wrapped her arms around my shoulders and pulled herself onto my lap, "or do you want to make some use of this empty theatre?"

For the record, I knew that was another dodge. A more sophisticated one admittedly, but still, obviously her changing the subject to avoid me asking more questions. I knew that quite clearly. I just didn't care.

Relationships are built on trust anyway, right?

A WERESTEED AT THE SLOTS

1.

MY GIRLFRIEND'S TRUCK HAD BALLS. NOT literal ones, of course, but chrome facsimiles that attached to the hitch. They looked strangely in place on her vehicle, which looked strangely in place enclosed around her as she drove me and my assistant down the sun-parched highway. It was a black pickup, enormous in size and decorated with polished chrome on the grill and interspersed periodically across the frame. She, on the other hand, was a medium-height blonde with muddy brown eyes, a low cut spaghetti-strap top, and faded blue jeans. If not for the gun strapped to her hip, she would have looked like the average southern belle. On second thought, I suppose the gun didn't disqualify her from fitting that stereotype.

"I'm still amazed by this glass," I said as I stared at the noonday sun from my seat on the passenger's side. A lesser man might have objected to the woman taking the wheel on such a long journey. A lesser man would also have been a stupider man, and one with a severe crotch injury to boot.

"Yeah, our R&D guys are something else," Krystal said, as she passed a motorist moving too slowly for her tastes, and by "too slowly," I mean "under ninety miles an hour."

"Assuredly. When did you get the glass put in, anyway?"

"Oh, I've always had it. I'm something of a fang junkie, so it only makes sense to keep it in my car."

"Ah . . . oh," I said. It really shouldn't have been surprising. Krystal worked for an agency of the government that dealt with supernatural beings on a daily basis. It wasn't farfetched that she would be seduced by the confidence and power of a vampire. Not one like me—a more classic, suave vampire.

"It's a joke, Freddy. You're my first light-allergic boyfriend. I promise," Krystal said with a wide, cheerful grin.

We both had good reason to be happy. Even though Krystal and I had begun dating after our high school reunion a few weeks back, we had only formalized our relationship as being committed a few days ago. I suppose that doesn't sound like much, but when the majority of your mortal life was spent cuddling up to a tub of ice cream and a classic film, getting a girlfriend still held something of a primordial thrill.

"I'm just glad we get to come," chimed Albert, from the back.

"Of course. I wanted you guys to come," Krystal said. "This is Thanksgiving, after all. It'll be a nice change to eat with friends instead of being camped out in some motel room on a stakeout, trying to figure out if the local murders are the work of a serial killer or a ghoul."

"We're glad to spend it with you," I said truthfully. This was my first Thanksgiving with other people in years, and I was all but brimming with joy in anticipation and appreciation. "Though, I'm still not sure why we'll be spending it in Vegas."

"There aren't many of us agents to go around, and when you take out the few who've managed to wrangle families along with their careers, there are even less. So while we get the holidays themselves off, we pretty much have to work right up until them. Besides, they have great restaurants and I can't cook for shit."

"Right, but why Vegas?" I asked again.

"I used to do life counseling for parahumans who were having trouble," Krystal said. "One of my old clients called and asked me to come out and advocate for him. Apparently, he got into trouble with the local dracolings."

"What's a dracoling?" Albert asked from the back. I was thankful he didn't know, because the truth was I certainly didn't either.

"Dracolings are basically humans with dragon blood. They're not much stronger physically than mortals, but those bastards have a touch of magic and are sly as foxes when it comes to money. Not to mention they own all of the casinos in Las Vegas," Krystal said, swerving past another motorist while throwing up the finger.

"That's impossible," I said. "Vegas is a town owned by many different corporations and investors. One group of people couldn't possess all of it."

"And no human would burn to a crisp just from a little sunlight. You want to crack open the door and see how things go?" Krystal asked.

"*Touché*." I sighed as I admitted defeat. Living as a vampire and dealing with Krystal had forced me to re-evaluate my definitions of what was and wasn't possible. It was rarely an enjoyable process to indulge in. "How exactly does this glass let in the light without reducing me to cinders?"

"Magic," Krystal said simply. "I'd go more in depth, but I'm not an arcane specialist. All I know is that they enchant the glass and my boyfriend can come along for the ride."

"And his assistant," Albert said, poking his face through ever-so-slightly from the backseat.

"And who could forget his charming assistant?" Krystal reassured him. Perhaps it was because of the way he died or maybe it was simply who he was, but Albert could be a bit insecure at times. Then again, I was the last person to be throwing stones in that regard.

"So, these dracolings, they own all of Vegas somehow. What does that have to do with your client?" I asked.

"Bubba has a bit of a gambling problem."

"Bubba?" I asked.

"Bubba?" Albert echoed.

"Bubba," Krystal affirmed. "And I'll thank you to be nice to him when you boys meet. He's a good guy and a sweetheart. Aside from the gambling problem, he's hard-working and responsible."

"Sounds as though the gambling might have gotten ahead of the other stuff," I said.

"It's the damn holidays," Krystal said. "If all you have is an addiction, then seeing everyone connecting with friends and family will leave you feeling lonely. So running off to the only thing that seems to give you joy and validation sounds like a good idea. It's a sad scenario, and I wish my agency was doing more to help it."

"Why aren't they?" I asked.

"Budget and manpower limitations. If we have to choose between putting down a revolution of mages and offering counseling to depressed pixies, guess where the funds end up?" Krystal said.

"I see," I said. "So, your friend Bubba was caught up in gambling, and since these dracolings own Vegas, I assume they acquired his debt?"

"More or less. Dracolings love gambling because they're good at it. They have sharp minds and sharper senses, so it's hard to get one past them," Krystal said.

"If they're so good, then why does anyone ever gamble with them?" I asked.

"Because they share their ancestor's weakness as well as their strength."

"They eat virgins?" Albert asked uncertainly.

"What? No. They can't resist a bet. If you play for high enough stakes and can trick them into betting on something you know you will win, then you can make a fortune."

"So, it's like playing the lottery, except instead of risking a dollar, you basically risk everything you own," I said.

"That's not the worst analogy I've ever heard. Anyway, they have a lot of treaties with my agency, and there's respect for us, so if I go in and advocate for Bubba, I should be able to at least get him on some sort of payment plan."

"I'm guessing I don't want to know what the other option for him is," I said.

"Smart man. His other option is working for them at minimum wage until he pays off his debt," Krystal said.

"He could always declare bankruptcy." Albert's voice was raised slightly, and there was a touch of pride in his tone. I had been teaching him some basic financial terms, and it seemed he was anxious to show he had listened.

"That works with human debt, but dracolings have special provisions that allow them to enslave people who are indebted to them," Krystal said. "It's actually not that far off from what happened with the Native American treaties, as far as cultural preservation goes, though dracolings had much better leverage and representation."

"What was their leverage?" I asked.

"Same as their representation. They called in a great grandparent to negotiate for them. Those negotiators agreed to help the country's war efforts in exchange for certain privileges. The result was that the dracolings got special areas with limited government interference and the right to keep their customs and traditions alive without sanction," Krystal said.

"Help with the war? This must have been a long time ago, was it World War One?"

"Las Vegas existed way before that, dear," Krystal said. "It's actually been around for centuries, though it didn't go the way of glitz and glamor until the last fifty years or so, when that became the best money-making campaign."

"For centuries . . . was it the civil war, then?" I tried again.

"Still too late. Parahumans were actually forced to align with the North during the Civil War, since their treaties and contracts were with the United States of America, and that's the title that the North retained. It's one of the reasons Lincoln knew he could win if the South seceded."

"Huh . . ." I sighed. "The things they leave out of the history books."

"In defense of 'them,' we're the ones who ordered those things stay out of the books," Krystal said.

"'We' being your employer," I said.

"Bingo," Krystal affirmed.

"How long has your non-existent little agency non-existed?" I asked.

"Since the beginning," she said. "We were formed at the same time the treaties and agreements with the various supernatural groups were, so that we could police and enforce those contracts."

"Wait a minute," Albert said, leaning up from the back seat. "When you say 'since the beginning,' do you mean . . . ?"

"It was a good deal all around. The supernatural creatures wanted a country where they had rights as citizens, and the founders of the country needed some way to drive back the superior numbers and might of the English."

"Are you telling me that vampires and werewolves are the reason America won the Revolutionary War?" I asked, dumbfounded.

"No, I'm saying America somehow managed to pull it out thanks to the French," Krystal scoffed.

There was a beat of silence, then Albert said: "You know, when you think about it, her version makes a lot more sense."

I shook my head. "The things you think you know."

"Be proud, Freddy, there were powerful vampires in that war," Krystal said. "They eliminated entire British platoons in a single night, saving the lives of American soldiers and civilians in the process."

"Yeah . . . but still," I said. "It's a lot to take in."

"I tell you what—once we get done with this business with Bubba and our Thanksgiving, I'll request clearance to show you a few files. I think getting in touch with your vampire heritage will do a lot for your pride as an Undead American," Krystal said, with a gentle tone I had forgotten she could use.

"That sounds surprisingly nice," I said. "You think things with Bubba and the dracolings will be that easy to deal with?"

"I'm sure of it," Krystal said.

One day, one beautiful and glorious day, I will stop listening when she says things like that.

2.

"OKAY, BOYS, THE NAME OF TODAY'S GAME is called Keep Your Mouth Shut," Krystal said as we took a seat at a long conference table. We had checked into our hotel—the Excalibur—upon arriving and were told to come straight to the meeting room. Our bags were swept away, and we were hustled down the hall into a pleasant-looking room that seemed suspiciously absent of cameras or windows. Krystal had attempted to protest that neither Albert nor I were a part of the meeting; however, the security said everyone who arrived with her had to show up, and do so immediately. She hadn't even been allowed to change into her business-appropriate attire; instead, she was stuck attending her meeting in dusty jeans and a red tank top. Thus, she was giving us a quick rundown of what we were to do during the meeting, which essentially consisted of not speaking a damn word.

"I'll talk to Morgan as soon as he comes in, but there is a chance you two will have to sit through the whole thing. Dracolings can be odd about stuff, and he might see you two as necessary additions just because you're with me. If that's the case, then stay quiet no matter what," she said.

"I don't think either of us would have anything to add, anyway," I said.

"You think that now, but . . . look, dracolings don't like when things change. They've been holding on to the same traditions for millennia. They might say something or do something that seems offensive to you modern guys. Deal with it. You have to stay quiet. Working with dracolings requires a two year long certification process that has to be renewed annually. That's how complicated interacting with them is."

"That seems a bit excessive," I said.

"These are people who have government protected rights to do things the way their traditions dictate, regardless of certain laws. Additionally, they are shrewd gamblers and place a tremendous amount of emphasis on a person's honor. Anything that is said to them is taken as a legally binding commitment. A poorly-timed joke could cost you your entire life savings. Still seem excessive?"

"Can I go to the room?" Albert asked. He was fidgeting and biting gently on his lower lip. I didn't blame him; Krystal had put a generous amount of fear into me too with her explanation.

"Hopefully, yes," Krystal said. "But if not, just remember to stay quiet. You can't make any mistakes if you don't say anything."

She likely had more to tell us, but at that moment it became too late. The doors opened, and four men walked into the room. Three of them wore suits that were clearly custom tailored by master craftsmen. Jewelry adorned them in ways that seemed just a touch elaborate on men, and each moved with an oddly fluid grace and supreme confidence. In one glance, I knew they owned this room, this building, and everything their eyes surveyed. These were leaders, men who would have been kings in another time and place. As they sat down across from us, folding themselves into the high-backed leather chairs, I finally tore my gaze away and looked at the other man who had entered the room.

He looked . . . different. This man stood at least a foot taller than the dracolings, and likely a hundred or so pounds heavier. His broad frame was clothed by a short-sleeved plaid shirt and a pair of jeans. A baseball cap hid his hair, but a pair of surprisingly kind eyes peered out from beneath its brim. His bulk was primarily muscle, though a gut did betray that at least some of his lifestyle was unhealthy. He gave a big grin and a small wave to Krystal, then took a seat a few spaces apart from the dracolings.

"Pleasant evening, Enforcer Jenkins," said the middle dracoling, an older man with jet black hair.

"Pleasant evening, Lord Ackers," Krystal said. She seemed composed, but colder than normal. Krystal always seemed to have a devil-may-care attitude about her, trusting her skill and smarts to see her through any trouble that life dished out. That was absent now; in its place were careful eyes and conservative body language. It was a very peculiar shift, and one that made me realize how much I preferred the everyday version of her.

"Before we begin our discussion on Mr. Emerson's debt, I would like to request permission to speak with you on a matter pertaining to the meeting itself," Krystal said.

The black-haired dracoling—Lord Ackers I suppose—leaned back in his chair for a moment and appeared to genuinely consider it. It seemed like a simple request to me, but I noticed the other dracolings looking at him anxiously. It was beginning to dawn on me that Krystal hadn't elaborated when she talked about how serious tradition and honor was when talking to these people.

"I will permit your request, on the condition that we may address each other informally," Lord Ackers said. "We have met together many times, and I see no reason why we should not be able to be familiar with one another."

Krystal hesitated for a moment, and then nodded. "I agree, Morgan. You and I have had dealings before."

"Excellent, Krystal. I prefer engendering comfort in those I work with regularly," Morgan said. Funny thing though, Krystal didn't seem any more comfortable now than she had been moments before. If anything, I was picking up more signs of stress from her body. I hoped that dracoling sight, hearing, and smell weren't on par with my own.

"Now, what would you like to speak of?" Morgan asked her.

"I would like to formally request that my two attendants be sent back to the hotel room," Krystal said. "They are not affiliated with the Agency, and as such, do not have clearance to be present at this meeting."

"Why not? The one wearing false glasses is a vampire, and the one wearing a T-shirt is a zombie. Both of them are parahumans and therefore are allowed to know of others of their kind," Morgan said. It was a bit creepy that he knew what Albert and I both were, and even that my glasses were fake.

"What you speak is true. However, this meeting involves the financial status of another person and his arrangement with you. Those are things that are considered private, and those not involved would not be privy to such information," Krystal countered.

"Yes, but the privacy control is all on our end," Morgan said with a small grin. "If I have no objection to their presence, then there is no legal need for them to vacate the room."

I braced for Krystal to tell him to shut up and just let us out of the damn meeting already. She wasn't known for her patience and an argument about keeping non-essential people around had to be taxing her limits. I was sure she would be lighting into this smug, suit-wearing jerk at any moment.

"You are correct, Morgan. I thank you for hearing my humble request. The matter has been satisfactorily concluded," she said. I don't think I kept much of the shock off my face. Krystal being subservient at all, let alone to this degree, was mind blowing.

"Good," Morgan said. "Now we move on to the matter of Mr. Emerson's debt. As of today, he owes us four hundred ninety-two thousand, eight hundred and sixty-two dollars. We have stopped counting the cents and begun rounding to the nearest dollar for convenience's sake."

"Four . . . hundred . . . *thousand*?" Krystal asked. Though her words were directed to Morgan, her eyes were digging straight into Bubba. I had seen those eyes before, and clearly Bubba had as well, since he was avoiding her gaze and looking very thoroughly ashamed. The man had every physical advantage over her, but it was evident he had a healthy amount of fear for this thin blonde woman, which only showed that he was much smarter than his name would indicate.

"Four hundred ninety-two thousand, eight hundred and sixty-two dollars, actually," Morgan corrected her. "As you know, this is well above the level where we are allowed to place him into our custody until he has worked off the debt. Additionally, he has passed the point where there is any legal recourse to adjust his debt or payment."

"I am aware of this now," Krystal said slowly. "Though, when Mr. Emerson requested my presence, it was with the indication that I would be acting as advocate. In matters over two hundred thousand, it is well known that no outside entity holds any authority to alter the decisions of the dracoling who holds that debt. I am a touch confused as to why, then, Mr. Emerson has asked me to come all the way out here."

"I cannot speak to that," Morgan said. "I do not claim to understand what goes on in Mr. Emerson's mind. However, I took your meeting because we strive to be in compliance with all clauses of our treaty with your government, and to try and foster good relations between us two."

"I thank you for accepting my meeting, and your good will is noted and will be reported. In the spirit of such good will, I have another boon to ask of you, Morgan, since it seems our meeting will be coming to a swift end. I would like to request that Mr. Emerson be permitted to tell both you and me why he felt it necessary to draw us into a meeting with no possibility of resolution," Krystal said in a strained voice. Her eyes were dead set on Bubba, who, for his part, seemed more resigned than nervous about his problematic situation.

"I daresay that would play directly into what he was hoping for," Morgan said. "I am not in the habit of aiding those who seek to waste my valuable time and resources."

"I would consider it a high token of friendship between your people and the Agency," Krystal said slowly, pronouncing every syllable with care and consideration. Given what she had told us, speaking on behalf of her office must have been exceedingly dangerous.

"Well, then, I would be a fool not to offer such a token," Morgan said, his grin deepening noticeably. "Mr. Emerson, you may speak with Krystal on the topic of why you called in an advocate for this case."

"I didn't call in an advocate," Bubba said, a snarky tone and southern twang reverberating in the strong bass of his voice. "I called in my friend."

Bubba turned his body and met Krystal's gaze. "I knew as soon as I lost my last bet that it was over. I just wanted to tell you goodbye in person. You were a lot of help to me after I lost Mom and Dad, and you helped keep me on the right track for a long time. You're the only person left in this world to miss me, and I just wanted to thank you for what you did. You're one of the few that cares, and I didn't want you to think you had failed me somehow when you heard about this. I wanted you to know that if you hadn't been there, I would have wound up in a much worse place much sooner. So, Krystal, for everything you did and for all the people I know you're going to go on to help, thank you from the bottom of my heart."

Bubba stood from his chair and looked back at the dracolings. "Okay, shitheads, we can go now."

"That concludes our meeting," Morgan said to Krystal as he rose. "I hope you enjoy your stay at the hotel, and please feel free to call on me if you have any other issues that need discussion." The other dracolings echoed his movements, and all four men began heading for the door.

"Wait!" Krystal yelped. She stood up from her chair and knocked it back. Her eyes were sparking and her jaw was set. This was a Krystal I was more familiar with. This was the Krystal who was about to whip some ass.

"I invoke the right to challenge for the debt of Bubba Emerson," she declared.

That's pretty much when all hell broke loose.

3.

BUBBA BELLOWED OUT A POWERFUL "NO!" and leapt forward. Before he had taken two steps, one of the dracolings touched his shoulder and Bubba dropped to the ground in wild spasms. Krystal . . . well, there's no other way to say it . . . Krystal growled gutturally and leapt to Bubba's shaking side. The other dracoling pulled Morgan away and stood between him and a now clearly pissed-off Krystal. Albert, meanwhile, let out a squeak and dropped from his chair to hide under the table. I desperately wanted to follow suit, but a part of me was screaming that if I dropped down and didn't keep my eyes trained on the altercation, there was a very good chance I would soon be single again. I knew I was physically stronger than everyone else in the room, but that didn't mean much when just the yelling was making me feel skittish.

It was Morgan who broke the silence. "Enforcer Jenkins, given Mr. Emerson's outburst and the sudden commotion, I am willing to acquiesce that I may not have heard you correctly. Would you be so kind as to repeat yourself?"

"I demand the right to challenge for the debt of Bubba Emerson," Krystal said softly as she held Bubba's shoulder while his twitching subsided.

"Acknowledged," Morgan said. "You are aware that, as a woman, you are ineligible to challenge in our traditional manner?"

"I am," Krystal agreed.

"Then we shall conduct the match using our secondary method. You may follow me," Morgan said, straightening his suit and not quite hiding the greedy glint in his eye.

"I request our stakes be held in escrow," Krystal said, rising slowly from Bubba's side.

Morgan nodded. "That is your right as well. Bubba Emerson shall stay with your attendants, but they shall remain within this casino. Are those conditions acceptable?"

"They are," Krystal said. "I will instruct my attendants on the handling of our stakes, and then we may begin the match."

"Acceptable." Morgan took a step back and waited against the wall. His attendants followed his cue, leaving the massive, dropped body of Bubba alone in the center of the floor.

Krystal hurried over to me. "This shouldn't take long, so as soon as Bubba wakes up, get him down to the restaurant. That shock will have taken a lot out of him, so get some food in him fast. I should be able to join you guys within the hour."

"I would very much like to be told what is going on," I said in a hushed whisper.

"I know, sweetie," Krystal said kindly. "And Bubba will fill in the gaps when he comes around. Just have some faith that I know what I'm doing 'til then, okay?"

"Of course. We'll take care of him, but please join us soon."

"No problem," she said, with her usual, confident grin. It was picture perfect, the heartwarmingly familiar image of Krystal about to lay waste to some unsuspecting fool who had dared to take her on. If only I hadn't heard her heart rate jump, or smelled the surge of fear that ran through her.

Sometimes, being a vampire really blows.

4.

"IT'S AN ANCIENT RITE," BUBBA SAID, as he began doing considerable damage to the steak resting innocently in front of him. I had hauled Bubba downstairs and found shelter in one of the buffets. It had taken him half an hour to come around, and as soon as he did, he had leapt up and sworn he would tear Morgan limb from limb. After that, it took us another ten minutes to calm him down—somewhat—when he realized Krystal had gone through with the challenge. Once we finally convinced him it was happening, he'd agreed to fill in Albert and I, but only after visiting the buffet table.

"Basically," Bubba continued, "those who are equal or better to the one enslaved may challenge for the ownership of the debt. If the challenger wins, they get the debt, and the slave is either set free or serves 'em. If the dracolings win, the challenger is assigned a debt equal to the original slave's, and they get enslaved too."

"So, Krystal just put her freedom on the line for you?" I had known something was up, but I had never imagined it went that deep.

"Yup," Bubba said. "Which is why you shoulda stopped her, dammit! I didn't call her down here to get caught up in my mess. I just wanted to say goodbye to someone who mattered, and that's a short list."

"I didn't know." Even to my ears, it seemed a lame defense. "Besides, have you ever seen anyone stop Krystal from doing something she was set on? Ever?"

"Well . . . no," Bubba admitted. "But that don't mean you can't try."

"I'm sorry." Albert was fidgeting with the pile of peas on his plate, not making eye contact with either of us. "Krystal had said how cunning they were, and when things got bad, I just panicked. I should have tried to stop her too."

There was something oddly disarming about Albert's apology. It brought how helpless we had all truly been into glaring light.

"It ain't your fault," Bubba said. "If it's anybody's fault, it's mine. I know that girl. I should have known she'd pull something crazy like this the minute I got her involved. I was being a self-absorbed jackass, and now she's in danger."

"What kind of danger?" I asked. "All they said was something about a match. What's happening right now, anyway?"

"Dracolings are big on tradition," Bubba said. "So they only have two forms of trials. Since Krystal's a girl, she'll be doing the one for those they don't consider to be warriors. They're playing a game of chess right now."

"Chess? That's it? I thought she'd be fighting a bear with a stick or something, with how serious everyone was," I said.

"I think I'd rather she was fighting the bear. At least then we'd know she'd be okay."

"Yeah, Krystal would come back with a new rug." Albert chuckled. It was pretty hard to imagine anything, animal or otherwise, getting the best of Krystal in a fight.

"So . . . what if she loses?" I didn't want to ask, but it seemed pointless to ignore the possibility.

"If she loses, she becomes bound to them, something they own. That means she works for them, does whatever they say, and is susceptible to their magic," Bubba told us.

"Is that what they did to you earlier?" Albert asked.

"Yeah, the fuckers could have just frozen me in my tracks, but dropping me like a sack of rotten potatoes is also an option they have," Bubba said.

"Why would they take the bet, though? As an agent, Krystal has training, experience, and cunning. Plus, she hung out with the chess team in high school. Doesn't that seem like a bad bet to the dracolings?" I asked, though I didn't bother explaining how I knew she had hung out with the chess team in high school. I did say we once ran in similar social circles, after all.

"Dracolings take all kinds of bets, usually because they have an ace up their sleeve," Bubba said. "I promise you, whoever she's playing is a chess master. That aside, they'd own an agent if she loses. Dracolings love power, connections, and leverage. Having someone they own in the Agency is a payoff they couldn't pass up—forget the odds."

"So, they think they can win," I said.

"They *know* they can win. They always know they can win. That certainty is probably their only weakness. The only way to beat them is to come totally out of left field."

"If anyone can do that, Krystal can," Albert said with force.

"Damn right," Bubba agreed.

"She is something amazing," I said. "How did you two meet, anyway?"

"I lost my parents when I was young and fell in with a couple of rough kids from the neighborhood.

Weresteeds don't get much respect from the outset in the supernatural community, and I was kind of an exceptional case even in that regard," Bubba told us.

"Weresteed?" Albert asked.

"Yeah, I turn into a horse."

"Okay, hang on," I said. "I sort of get the werewolf thing. But horses? How does that even work? Horses don't bite people. Where would werehorses have originally come from?"

"Weresteeds." Bubba's tone was surprisingly firm as he corrected me. "And no, we don't bite people. It's passed on through lineage, like lots of other supernatural abilities. As for where we came from . . . I have no idea."

"You don't?" I asked.

"Do you know how vampires were created?" Bubba shot back.

"I suppose I don't, actually."

"Exactly. Parahumans ain't that special. We get to wonder about the origins of our kind just like the humans do. Maybe some of the really old ones might have an inklin' or two, but if anyone knows for sure, they ain't talkin'."

"I guess that does make sense," I said.

"I know where I came from," Albert announced.

"You know the source and details of the magic that pumps through your body, keeping your undead butt moving?" Bubba asked.

"Oh . . . no," Albert said.

"You see what I mean, then," Bubba said, polishing off the last of his steak. "Anyway, the point was that weresteeds don't get much respect, so I was working triple hard to make a street name for myself. I got busted one night, and Krystal was the one they sent down to deal with me. Instead of just beating me down, or putting me in a cage, she took an interest in me. She got me a part-time job, found me a real place to stay, and helped get me on my feet. If not for Krystal, I'd still be some idiot kid on the streets."

"That's pretty ama . . . zi . . ." I trailed off as a familiar scent hit my nostrils. Within moments, I had picked out the footsteps that corresponded to the smell I'd noted and could tell they were coming toward us. "Company," I said. Albert stiffened, and Bubba cracked his knuckles.

The dracoling—one of Morgan's nameless attendants—glided up to our table, showing no surprise that we were waiting for him.

"Gentlemen, if you will accompany me to the conference room. The match is done, and it is time for the winner to claim their prize." With that, the dracoling turned and began heading out of the restaurant.

"Do we go?" Albert asked.

"No option," Bubba said, as he finished a long draw of tea from his glass. "You heard him. It's time to settle up. Let's just hope things came out in our favor."

5.

FILTERING BACK INTO THE ROOM FELT ODD. Things had been so hurried and wild when we left, yet, when we entered the room, it was quiet and calm. Morgan and his attendants sat on the same side of the table, hands crossed and neutral expressions on their faces. The only blatant difference in the room was that Krystal was sitting on the same side of the table as the dracolings. Before I smelled her, before I heard her heartbeat, before I even saw her face, that fact alone told me all I needed to know.

"You lost," I said simply. I hadn't even made it to my chair. Albert, Bubba, and I were still near the door. I probably should have just walked in and taken a seat. I know I should have let Bubba do all the talking, since he was already in deep. But I didn't. Instead, I blurted out those words, because I didn't want to dance around the truth. I needed to know, right then and right there, standing by that doorway.

"Perceptive," Morgan said. "But not surprising for one of your ilk. Yes, Enforcer Jenkins did not triumph in her match and is now one of my belongings."

The word "belongings" grated against something inside me. I couldn't tell you what it was because it felt raw and hard, and those were things I wasn't accustomed to discovering in myself. Bubba apparently echoed my sentiment, though, as I heard his knuckles crack behind me.

"Now, now, no need for posturing," Morgan said with a slimy smile. "Mr. Emerson is already under our power, and while you two gentlemen do possess more physical strength than we do, I think you will find Enforcer Jenkins and Mr. Emerson harmed quite brutally should you attempt to escalate our little confrontation."

I could feel Bubba's tense body slacken. I doubted he had any concern for his own safety, but if they were going to hurt Krystal, then he wouldn't fight back. As for me, the idea of throwing a fit hadn't even occurred to me. I had an entirely different backup plan ready for this situation.

"I demand the right to challenge for the debt of Krystal Jenkins and Bubba Emerson," I stated loudly.

Hell didn't really break loose this time. Krystal did gasp, and Bubba seemed a touch surprised, but the dracolings only laughed at me.

"You are a silly little vampire, aren't you?" Morgan asked. "First off, you are not an agent nor a knight, so you have no rights to challenge. Secondly, you cannot challenge for the debt of two slaves. One warrior, one slave—that is the way the bets are structured."

"What if he doubled up?" Albert said.

Morgan raised an eyebrow. "Explain."

"Fred will bet his freedom . . . and mine. It will be one battle, but if he wins, he gets both slaves. If you win, you get two new slaves. The rules are the same. We're just raising the stakes," Albert said, not without some hesitation.

"You can't do that," I whispered.

"And you can? Fred, if I can't work for you, they'll put me back in the ground anyway. You doing this is an unlife or death bet for me regardless. At least like this, they might take it."

"You gentlemen are aware we can hear you, correct?" Morgan asked. "And while I do find the raising of the stakes acceptable, I still have no reason to take the bet. Neither of you can demand a challenge, so it must be agreed on to be accepted. Yes, gaining two undead servants would have some use to us, but nowhere near as great as ownership of an agent. The potential gain is simply not great enough to justify the potential loss."

"Well, if it sweetens the pot any, I do own my own accounting agency. Maybe I could be used to help with the books," I said in desperation. It was a stupid long shot. I was under no illusions that the dracolings would actually find a vampire a more desirable bet because he was an accountant.

As it turned out, I was dead wrong in that assumption. It was like I'd jolted each of the dracolings with electricity, the way they reacted when I mentioned the word "accounting."

"You are . . . an accountant?" Morgan asked.

"Um, yes. I run my own business out of my apartment, and I do pretty good work," I said.

"Do you know how difficult it is to find a parahuman that is both capable and willing to balance books?" Morgan asked me again.

"I'm sure there are plenty of humans who are glad for the work," I said.

"Humans, bah!" Morgan said. "Due to secrecy agreements in our treaties, we can never reveal to them what we are, so any expenses incurred that relate to our nature must be hidden from them, forcing us to do the work ourselves."

"So, if you won Fred, you wouldn't have to do that anymore," Albert said. "You would finally have a parahuman who could do all of the numbers work for you."

"Indeed," Morgan said. "May I ask your full name, vampire?"

"Fredrick Frankford Fletcher."

"Well, Mr. Fletcher, in light of your occupation, I will admit that I do find this bet to be enticing," Morgan said. "It is accepted; however, our champion is currently out of the casino this evening. Would you be willing to wait until tomorrow morning to have your match?"

"How are they out of the casino?" I asked. "Krystal just had her match."

Morgan chuckled. "Mr. Fletcher, Enforcer Jenkins had a match with me, which was a game of chess. It is the trial used for women, since they are not strong enough to endure a man's trial. As a man, you will of course be doing battle in our traditional form."

Krystal had warned me they were stuck in the past. "Wait, so I won't be playing chess?" I'd been something of a chess champion in my youth, and I still played online to keep my mind fresh. I had been certain I could handle anything some dracoling could throw at me on the checkered battlefield. If that wasn't the contest, though, my confidence was somewhat lower. And by "somewhat," I mean "extremely."

"You will do battle with our champion in the manner our dragon ancestors faced. Of all the menaces in the land, only knights conducted themselves with the honor, strength, and determination to allow our ancestors to acknowledge them as worthy warrior combatants. As such, our trial is the one that the knights themselves used," Morgan said.

"Okay, so just so we're all on the same page here, what did I just sign up for?" I asked.

"Tomorrow morning, you will be battling our champion in a joust," Morgan said. "You may have access to our stables and equipment until then to prepare as needed. You may also use any steed on the premises, with, of course, the exception of the gray mare that our champion rides. Be in the stables at seven sharp, ready to compete."

"What about Krystal? Do we get to keep her in escrow?"

"You have no more neutral parties to entrust her to. All of you are involved in this wager," Morgan said. "Therefore, she will stay at my casino and under my attendant's watchful eye. Since Mr. Emerson's debt is still in question, our previous agreement to escrow remains valid, and he may stay with you. See you in the morning, Mr. Fletcher." With that, he gave us a wave toward the door. I looked at

Krystal before turning around, something I hadn't dared to do the entire time I had spoken with Morgan, for fear she would somehow talk me out of it.

When I did meet her eyes at last, I was nearly knocked back. They were all but screaming at me, her face contorted in frustration as she tried to communicate. I had known Krystal for a long time in my youth, and I had seen much of her since we reconnected, so I knew one thing for certain. Krystal could never have restrained her mouth if she felt that strongly about something, which left only one option—they had used their magic to render her silent.

Terrified as I was, I turned on my heel and strode out as powerfully as I could. There was no way I would let these bastards know I was shaking in my comfortable brown loafers.

6.

"YOU REALLY SCREWED THE POOCH ON THIS one," Bubba said, once we were comfortably far from the conference room and heading toward the stables. Though it would be foolish to assume the dracolings wouldn't have eyes and ears on every inch of their property, there was no sense in making our conversations easier for them to overhear.

"Maybe it will be okay," I said, more out of desperate hope than actual optimism. "I mean, a joust is sort of a physical event, and I am a lot stronger than humans."

"A joust is closer to a shooting match than a fight," Bubba corrected. "You have to aim your lance at a precise spot to try and topple your opponent, while steering your horse at just the right pace and keeping your balance, all while dodging the lance heading straight for you. The only place strength really comes in is in lifting the damn lance, which I'm sure you'll do great at."

We reached the gaming floor then, and after some quick directions from an attendant, headed to the arena. Evidently, Morgan had already called down and alerted everyone to our new level of clearance because, as we left the casino area and stepped into Excalibur's arena, not one worker stopped or bothered us. In fact, a pair of well-muscled men wearing suits let us into the arena, and then locked the doors after we stepped through. We kept silent as we moved past them, because the last thing we wanted was for everyone to see that we knew how good and screwed we were.

"It still doesn't seem hopeless," Albert said, once the doors had been secured behind us. "Vampires are more than strong; they also have enhanced coordination, reflexes, and speed."

"The key word there is 'enhanced,'" Bubba said, as we walked through the spacious tournament floor. Stadium seats stretched far above us, and the ground beneath us was covered in dirt and straw. On one side of the seating, in the center, there was a boxed off area adorned with curtains and jewels, a pair of thrones resting inside it.

"If Fred had been some sort of fighter, or athlete, or anything like that before he got turned, we might be a little better off," Bubba continued. "But given that he's wearing glasses and a sweater vest *after* becoming a vamp, I'm guessing he wasn't much of a tough guy when he had a heartbeat."

They both paused and looked at me, at which point I did my best to look inconspicuous. It wasn't as though I could really debate Bubba on that point.

"He still got enhanced, though," Albert said.

"And if I multiply ten by two, I get twenty. Much higher than two, but not as good as if I'd multiplied ten by ten and gotten a hundred," Bubba said. "Anyway, this is all pointless. Do you really think Morgan and his boys don't know vampires are stronger than dracolings? Dracolings always take bets they know they can win, so you can be damned sure there's an ace in the hole."

"What do you think it will be?" I asked.

"Oh, I don't wonder. I already know what it is," Bubba said. "Follow me."

With that, he began walking off across the arena, toward a set of large wooden doors near the rear. Albert and I kept pace, unsure of what to expect. Bubba reached the doors and threw them open with ease. He strode into a room that would have been dark to human eyes, though Albert and I could easily make out the horses resting comfortably in their stables. We ventured after him, and that's when the world came tumbling down.

The moment my foot crossed the threshold of the dark room, a cacophony of screaming noise pierced my ears. And let me tell you something—having senses beyond the human threshold isn't always a blessing. As the horses began to buck and kick and whinny in their stables, my ears overloaded, and I stumbled backward . . . backward into peaceful silence. Just as fast as the horses' tirade had begun, it ended.

"Whoa," Albert said.

"Vampires spook horses. Bad," Bubba said as he emerged from the stables. "You bloodsuckers are some of the ultimate predators, and a horse's senses are finely tuned to that sorta thing. Hell, even I get goose bumps when I stand too close to you."

"So, I can't ride one?" I asked, still trying to get my mental feet back under me.

"You won't even be able to stay in the same room as one. The minute you're in there, every nerve and sense that poor horse has will go haywire. Since you're strong, you'll probably be able to subdue one and climb on top of it, but riding it with any real control? You can forget that shit right here, right now."

"Bastards," Albert said.

"Maybe, but this might work to my advantage," I said. "I mean, their guy will be riding a horse too. Won't my being there spook his horse as well? At least I can put us on an even playing field."

"Yeah! Good thinking." Albert was clearly on board, but Bubba was already shaking his head.

"Dragon magic," he said simply. "They have control over their possessions, including their horses. You being there will surely spook their guy's horse, but it won't matter. He'll just override its fear. I told you already; the damn dracolings think of everything. You have to come out of left field."

"Well . . . what about you?" Albert said. "Can you turn at will, or are you only a full-moon shifter?"

I briefly wondered why I hadn't hit on that idea, but seconds later I became quite glad that Albert had beaten me to it. In a motion that was shockingly fast given his height and bulk, Bubba snapped Albert off the ground by the neck and held him several feet in the air.

"Now, I know," Bubba growled, "that you are *not* suggesting Fred ride me. I am positive you would not insult me and my kind so blatantly as to suggest I submit myself to bearin' a rider. Am I wrong?"

Albert shook his head as vigorously as he could with his neck being held in a hand the size of a ham, and Bubba dropped him to the ground. In truth, there was little Bubba could have done to hurt or injure Albert.

Raised zombies are a ridiculously hardy lot, but Albert hadn't been dead all that long, and he still hadn't gotten used to things like not fearing death. He and I were similar in that regard. The difference was that I was ever so slowly learning to pick my battles.

"He's right, you know," I said. "If you can turn at will, then you're probably the only chance we really have."

Bubba turned on me, and for a second, I thought he was going to throttle me too. His eyes were big, and there was a vein bulging in his neck. Knowing I was stronger than him didn't do much to cut the fear of having a giant man stare at me that way, so I finished my proposal with extra haste.

"It's the only chance Krystal has too."

It was like I'd stuck a pin in a balloon. Bubba's sudden ferocity slipped away like mercury running off a table, leaving me looking at a large, proud, powerful man who suddenly seemed very tired and unsure.

"I can turn at will, but it's one of the highest dishonors for a weresteed to be ridden like a common horse," Bubba protested weakly.

"Don't think of me as a rider," I said. "Think of me as a partner. Or think of me as a friend you're doing a favor for. I don't really care what title we put on it, as long as it gives us a fighting chance of winning our freedom back."

"You know, pride aside, it seems like the dracolings would have remembered that Bubba was a weresteed," Albert said. "That makes the whole horse thing just a small pain in the ass instead of a deal breaker. I mean, they even gave him his freedom on casino grounds so he could work with us. Weird."

I blinked in surprise. He was right. They had to know that Bubba would consent to being ridden if it meant saving Krystal and himself. Which meant there was something we were still missing.

"Actually, I think I can guess why they didn't count me as an option," Bubba said with a sigh. "I told you I was in a different situation than most weresteeds. Well . . . you know what? Just watch."

As I kept my eyes trained on him, Bubba seemed to ripple, like a pond a stone had just been chunked into. His skin became darker, and his hands grew hard as his fingers merged together. His eyes became huge as his face elongated. His body shifted, and a small popping sound registered to my ears as his clothes unsnapped. It seemed everything he wore was designed to snap off without tearing when he turned. I suppose that would be something of a must for a shape-shifter on a budget.

It sounds as though it took some time, but that is only through my own amped up perception. In truth, mere seconds passed between Bubba telling us to watch and Albert and I gazing upon a beautiful black-haired steed. It seemed strong and powerful, the kind of horse that made other horses slink back to their stables and munch on an oat bag rather than occupy the same track as such a beast. There was really only one problem.

"You're a pony!" Albert shrieked in odd delight. He was right though. Massive as Bubba was in human form, he was somewhat less imposing while hooved. He came up to maybe my waist, and my figure was not one of height and intimidation. Albert raced over and began stroking Bubba the Horse's head. There was a sound like a rubber band snapping, and Bubba was back in his normal form, immediately gathering up his clothes.

"So," I said, to gently broach the subject once Bubba's pants were back on.

"He's right," Bubba said curtly. "I'm a pony. I'm thirteen hands high, which makes me a big damn pony, but still a hand short of being a horse. Joust horses are supposed to be the biggest of the breed, so they can bring more power and height for their rider. If we use me, then we've as good as lost."

"Maybe," I said. "But then again, I'm not anyone's ideal jouster. I took this bet because I'm really good at chess, which is ultimately the same thing as saying I'm bad at everything physical."

"So, we're double fucked?" Bubba asked.

"Probably," I admitted. "We have to try, though. I mean, I hate sports, and competition makes me a little nauseous, and the idea of physically engaging with someone turns my legs to jelly. But what other choice do we have?"

"We'll get our asses kicked," Bubba said.

"I've gotten my ass kicked a whole lot of times. One more probably won't kill me. Besides, at least with a steed that won't buck me, we have a shot at getting lucky."

Bubba chuckled. "A vampire riding a pony. It certainly does come out of left field."

"So, what now?"

"Now, we practice. We've only got a few hours before we're all slaves for life."

7.

"HOW'S IT LOOKING OUT THERE?" I ASKED as Albert came scurrying back into our stable. We'd discovered that the stables on the opposite of the arena were empty of horses and used for equipment, so we'd set up shop there to get gear for the match. We'd spent several hours riding and getting comfortable with the lance, and had made some key discoveries: Bubba's height really was a detriment, my aim was another, and it was damn hard to find a saddle that would fit a pony in a stable stocked for jousting horses.

"Pretty full," Albert said. People had been filtering in for nearly an hour, and sooner or later, we'd be called out into the arena. Some casino workers had given us the rundown a few hours previously. Apparently, we would be called onto the floor to make introductions. Then Morgan would explain the rules, and we would bow to one another. And then the fight would start. I guess I wasn't surprised a shrewd businessman like Morgan was filling the seats for the show; I just hoped that didn't mean I was in deep shit if I did something supernatural. If only Krystal were here, I could have asked her who was responsible for secrecy in this situation.

I felt a pang in my stomach when I thought about Krystal. It seemed like every time I'd wound up in this scenario before, she'd rushed in and saved me somehow. A part of me had expected her to come into the arena last night and explain how she'd worked everything out, how we could go home. Sitting there, wearing rusty armor and holding a large wooden lance, it finally sank in all the way. Krystal wasn't coming to our rescue this time. Today, the only cavalry we had was a werepony, a bumbling zombie, and a chickenshit vampire.

I wondered if it was too late to place a bet on the other guy to win.

"You got a good grip on your lance?" Albert asked.

"Huh?" I said, yanking myself out of my reverie. "Oh, yeah, it feels just like holding a baseball bat."

"When did you ever play baseball?"

"I tried out for the team in high school. Didn't do so well," I said, purposely keeping my answer brief. No need to go into details about accidently whacking the coach in the balls when the bat slipped out of my hands.

"Fred," Albert said. "Do your best."

"I'll give it my all, however much that's worth."

"Contestants, please report to the arena!" A loud voice thundered through our stable, indicating it was time for the match to begin. Albert hustled over to the doors and worked them open. They were a touch rusty, so it took a few moments before they were wide enough for Bubba and me to exit through. As a result, the dracoling champion was already out in the arena, garnering cheers and roses from the fans. He was a strapping young man, long blond hair and large physique under his glistening armor. There was no way he was stronger than me, but from the way he moved across the arena on his horse, it was clear I could have ridden for ten years and not had the same equestrian ability he possessed. My only hope was that he was worse with a lance than he was on horseback, and that was, admittedly, a very dim hope.

Bubba whinnied and began moving forward, pulling us out into the sight of the crowd. I'd expected the noise to suddenly stop, like a needle on a record, but instead it grew larger. With laughter. I'll admit, we did look fairly humorous, but as I felt Bubba tense beneath me, I put my hand on his head to steady him. I turned it delicately to where the throne box was located. Morgan sat in one of the gaudy chairs, wearing a lavish tunic and drinking from a jeweled goblet. In the other, wearing a scoop neck dress and an angry scowl, was Krystal. He'd dressed her up like a medieval Barbie just to prove that he could. Bubba stamped the ground once and loosened his muscles, telling me he understood. These people didn't matter; their laughter wasn't important. The only thing we needed to focus on was saving our friend.

"Good morn, my loyal subjects," Morgan bellowed to the crowd. "Today, we hold a joust for the hand of my own beautiful Lady Jenkins. Standing to the east, representing your king, please greet Sir Galvin!" The laughter decreased as the cheering was turned up a few notches.

"And to the west, representing himself, I present to you: Fred!"

"I think I got shafted on that introduction," I muttered to Bubba as the waves of laughter and pointing increased. I almost wished I had worn a helmet to cover my face and hide my shame, but Bubba had pointed out that it could obscure my vision. Besides, it's not like a lance to the face was going to do any damage to my head.

"Now, my dear subjects, this match shall go to the first opponent with three points. A broken lance anywhere on the body counts as a single point. And, as always, should a rider be knocked to the ground in any way, he has lost the match," Morgan said. "If our jousters will bow to one another . . . ." I inclined my body as best I could in armor, and, across the arena, Galvin did the same. "Excellent, now take your positions."

Bubba trudged over to the railing that ran through the center of the arena. We took our place on the right side and waited as Galvin took his, on the left. It took him longer despite his superior skill, since he insisted on walking sideways and blowing kisses to the ladies in the audience. I noticed he threw several extra air smooches at Krystal and tightened my grip.

A small man dressed in period clothes came to the center of the railing and checked to see that we were both in position. He took a few steps back, and then, with a jerking motion, waved his flag and told us to charge.

I wish I could tell you it was over in a flash, that I don't remember what happened, but thanks to my damn vampire senses, I saw the whole thing clearly. Bubba was off like a shot; his size did not diminish the considerable power that being a werecreature afforded him. Galvin was moving quickly too, though his horse's size and power nearly broached the speed gap. As we approached each other, I focused on his chest, visualizing it as one of the rings I had practiced with all night. I steadied my lance and drove it right for his sternum.

In a motion as fluid as running water, Galvin rolled his own lance in a circle, knocking against mine to deflect it and arriving back at the perfect position to skewer me dead center, smashing his lance and nearly driving me off Bubba. The only thing that kept me seated was the ludicrous amount of strength in my legs, strength that had been of no help when he'd used simple physics to remove my leverage and redirect my thrust.

As Bubba slowed to a trot, I became vaguely aware of the loud cheers coming from the crowd. I righted myself and adjusted my seat as an attendant rushed forward with another lance.

It had been unreal; I'd never even had a chance at striking Galvin. He'd read my movements like a book and reacted to them perfectly, all of which was made easier by the difference of several feet in height between us. I looked across the arena to see him being handed another lance, smiling freely. For a moment, I wondered why he hadn't bothered to put a helmet on either. Then it hit me—he knew he didn't need one. If I'd had any sense of pride left at that moment, it might have been crushed.

Bubba and I pulled into position at the railing, and I took a deep breath to try and steady my nerves. I knew I didn't actually need to breathe, of course, but stimulus response is ingrained deeply in the human mind, even after death. It worked too, and I felt myself gain more control. I knew if I used the few advantages I did have, I'd be able to strike Galvin dead center. The attendant came out again and waved the flag, and Bubba and I surged forward, bent on destroying our opponent.

A few seconds later, we were trotting up the other side with a new dent in my armor and another unbroken lance lying on my side of the arena. It was no good. Galvin was just too well trained at this for me to overcome him with a few physical advantages and a night of practice.

Albert rushed to my side. “Fred! Fred, are you okay?”

“Well, I’m trying to get used to the idea of living and working in Vegas for the rest of my life, but other than that, I’m peachy,” I said as I pulled myself up.

“Yeah, you’re not doing too good,” Albert agreed.

“No, I am not.” I looked up into the throne box. Krystal was staring down at me, looking . . . I wasn’t sure. I didn’t think I had ever seen such a look on her face. It was desperation, sadness, and helplessness all rolled into one and smothered with guilt. She knew we were going to lose. So did Morgan and the audience. Hell, for that matter, even we knew we were going to lose.

“Guess we didn’t come far enough out of left field.” Albert sighed resolutely.

I paused for a moment, looking up at Krystal, then at Albert, then Bubba, working very hard to remember something Morgan had said earlier, word for word. A light clicked on in my head, and I had a plan. Go figure; I was tweaked out and amped up physically thanks to my vampire status, but the thing that might actually save us was my good old steel-trap of a memory.

"Get me a lance," I told Albert. As he hustled off to take the lance from an approaching attendant, I began working on my armor. After messing with the buckles for a few frustrating seconds, I gave up and just tore the armor off. I stretched my limbs, and then leaned into Bubba.

"Can you run faster than you have been?" Bubba stamped once, indicating "yes" in the code we'd worked out during our training. "Good," I told him. "Do that. Run as fast and as hard as you can. Stay straight along the rail no matter what. And try to trust me, because I think we're about to go for broke."

Bubba stamped his hoof three times, which meant, if I was remembering correctly, "Let's go beat these bitches." (What? It had been a long night, and we'd had a bit of fun with the code.)

Albert came scampering back and handed me my lance. "Where's your armor?"

"I don't need it for this one," I said.

"Okay . . . why not?"

"Because if we keep trying the same thing, we'll definitely lose, so at least this way we have a one-percent chance of winning."

"I kind of figured that," Albert said. "I meant, why don't you need armor for whatever you're trying?"

"Just watch," I said with a sigh. Bubba moved slowly into our starting position, and I checked my legs in the saddle to make sure they were just where I wanted them. Galvin hesitated to take his spot, staring across at me as I sat sans armor on the back of my pony. He reached up to the tip of his lance and broke off a chunk of the wooden tip. Then he smiled at me and began riding to his starting position. The meaning wasn't lost on me. Right now, he was essentially holding a giant wooden stake, and if he hit me this time, I'd be nothing but a pile of dust on the floor.

I tried very, very, *very* hard to keep the sudden rush of fear that hit me from showing on my face. I hadn't expected him to raise the stakes (no pun intended), and in truth, if I'd known Galvin was going to do that, I likely would have just taken the final blow and lost the match. That option wasn't on the table though, so all I could do was take another stabilizing breath and pray.

The starter attendant jerked his flag, and we were off.

My first thought was that Bubba really hadn't lied about holding back. That black little pony was thundering down the track like it was a mini-horse of the apocalypse. I was ninety-percent certain that if I'd been able to turn back and look, I would have seen hoof prints in the ground from how hard he was striking it.

Galvin noticed the difference too, and began spurring his own steed vigorously to match pace. It was all for naught, though. His horse might have had more size, but Bubba was a pissed off weresteed running all out. That meant the only advantages Galvin still had were the height of his horse and his skill with a lance.

As I pulled up my legs and secured my balance, I took away his height advantage the only way I could think of. I stood up on Bubba's back, riding him like several hundred pounds of angry, charging surfboard. It was a precarious position, and if I'd been human, there was no chance I could have pulled it off. But being a vampire isn't all sun allergies and blood dependency. Still, even with my balance it was a challenge, but it was one I could handle for a short while. And with the way Bubba was closing the gap between Galvin and me, I wouldn't need to keep it up for long.

My antics had taken the crowd and, more importantly, Galvin by surprise. Unfortunately, as we drew nearer, any uncertainty slid off his face, leaving only focused determination in its place. This man was truly a warrior, and even with the advantage of speed and the leveling of our heights, there was no chance I'd be able to best him in a joust.

Luckily, he didn't know that I was no longer competing in the joust. I'd moved on to a more modern game.

The two of us drew within lance range, and Galvin waited the split second to deflect my thrust. That thrust never came, though. I kept both hands locked on the lance raised on my right side, but made no movements to aim it at Galvin's body. In a fraction of a second, Galvin read the course of my lance and knew I wasn't aiming for him. I'm not sure if he paused to wonder why, or simply didn't care, but he aimed that giant stake at my heart without hesitation and went for the kill.

My left hand smashed against his lance, leaving my own weapon and protecting my heart by pushing his blow over my shoulder. Disappointment smeared across his handsome face as he realized it would take another run to bring me down, but there was no fear or wonderment. We were too close for me to hit his heart with my lance. As our eyes met in the moments before we were even with one another, he saw the arch my arm was moving in, and comprehension dawned across his face. I was impressed he'd figured it out.

With every ounce of power I could pull from my one arm of undead muscles and the momentum of Bubba's run, I swung my lance like a baseball bat and sent it smashing into Galvin. The force of my blow sent him flying off his horse and several feet away, and it seemed to knock over the horse as well. Unfortunately, it also sent me twirling around, losing my footing and tumbling over. I bounced off Bubba's back and grabbed uselessly for something to hold on to. As I started to lift into the air on the rebound, I wondered if I could make a case that Galvin had fallen first. Before I could fully commit myself to losing, I felt a sharp pain in my shoulder as something grabbed hold and pulled me back onto the pony. Glancing upward, I saw it was Bubba himself who had pulled me up, rearing his head back and chomping into my flesh. I'd never been happier to have someone surprise me with an attack.

The arena greeted me with the dead silence I'd expected when Bubba and I first came out, as they decided what to make of the final round. I'd unseated their champion, but in a way they'd never seen nor dreamt of before. At last, one man in the top row began clapping, and like a landslide the applause and cheering began pouring down upon us.

I leaned over to my trusty steed and whispered, "We should both be very thankful I'm no longer physically capable of pissing myself in fear. Otherwise, we would have been doused."

Bubba stamped once.

8.

"YOU CANNOT POSSIBLY EXPECT THAT ludicrous spectacle to count as a victory!" Morgan hollered as we entered his conference room. "That wasn't jousting at all. It was a circus act!"

"'Should a rider be knocked to the ground in any way, he has lost the match,'" came a female voice from behind him. "A direct quotation from the rules you set down, Lord Ackers. Fred was still on top of his horse, while Galvin was gasping on the ground. Fred won, or does this conversation not serve as adequate proof?"

Krystal stepped forward from her place at the rear of the room, still wearing the dress but sporting her old ass-kicking grin as an accessory. "Your magic can't keep me silent anymore because you don't own me, or any of us. You bet, and you lost."

She strode over and gave me a large kiss on the cheek. "I have to admit, Freddy, you caught me by surprise."

"We'll list gymnastic miracles as things we're thankful for at lunch today," I said. "Now, can we please get out of here?"

"Yes, get out," Morgan spat bitterly. "None of you are welcome in my hotel any longer. Your things will be waiting at the front desk."

"No worries," Krystal said with a smile. "Lord Vestrin owns the Bellagio, and I think he'll welcome us with open arms after hearing how we aided in your humiliating loss today."

Morgan's face grew white as he clenched his fists with rage. I began to realize that dracolings could handle a lot of things with casual calm, but losing bets and face were certainly not on that list.

"Oh, before we go, though, there is one last piece of business to attend to," Krystal said, walking back over to Morgan.

"And what is that?" Morgan asked, a sneer firmly affixed to his sour face.

Krystal gave him a large grin, and then drilled her knee directly into his groin. Morgan let out a guttural gasp and crashed to the ground, his attendants surging forward to help him as the bodyguards made a beeline for Krystal. Bubba took two steps forward and cracked his knuckles, while I opened my mouth and allowed my fangs to extend. I was useless in a real fight, but after today, they didn't know that. The bodyguards reconsidered just how much they needed this job and backed off as Krystal turned and strode out the door. We followed quickly, pausing only as Krystal turned back to toss a final word to Morgan over her shoulder.

"Next time you tell me to be seen and not heard, I won't just kick them, I'll take them home as my fucking trophies."

"Can I just say how much I love this town for being anti-sunlight?" We were sitting at the table of yet another buffet while Krystal and Bubba plowed their way through a Thanksgiving smorgasbord. The truly shocking part was that Krystal was keeping pace with our gigantic new friend. "I mean, it's noon, and there's not a shred of natural light anywhere in this building. Plus, there are underground lots for us to park in. It's great. I feel great."

"Maybe you feel great because you finally got to put the smack down on someone." Krystal laughed. "My little Freddy is all grown up. This mean you're going to hang up your calculator and turn into a real ass-kicking vampire?"

"I somehow doubt it," I said. "Today was . . . well, let's call it a fluke."

"What do you mean?" Krystal asked. "You were awesome! I know you always say you can't stand physical confrontation, but you floored that douchebag without hesitation."

"I wouldn't say 'without hesitation,'" I protested. "I just used a visualization method to get my mind working in a more proper alignment with what my body needed to do."

"What the hell are you trying to say here?" Bubba asked, looking up from a huge rack of ribs.

"Um . . . at the last moment, I closed my eyes and pretended he was a baseball," I admitted.

There was a beat of silence, and then horror as everyone realized I was serious. The tension was broken first by Krystal's unrestrained laughter, then Bubba's, then Albert's, and finally my own, joining in for no other reason than that we were finally safe, and I could laugh without fear.

"You know, I have to admit that does make a lot more sense," Krystal said as her laughter died down to mere giggles. "I was wondering how Freddy finally found the balls to whack the crap out of someone. Now I know. All the balls were in his head."

"Don't sell him too short," Bubba said. "After all, he went into the final run planning on doing it, even if he had to cheat a bit to pull off the execution."

"True. Even that's a big step for Freddy."

"Never underestimate what a man will do to protect the people he cares about," Bubba said, with just a hair too much intensity.

"I won't." Krystal answered, with a rare tone of sincerity.

"Right . . . well, then I could go for some ice cream," Bubba said quickly, as he seemed to realize the direction our conversation had taken. "Albert, whaddya say we hit the sundae bar?"

"But I don't need to eat," Albert half-heartedly protested.

"And I don't need to drink beer, but that sure as shit ain't stopped me. Now, come on, zombie boy," Bubba said, all but picking Albert up and dragging him across the buffet.

"I think someone might have a crush," I said when Bubba was gone.

"You noticed? I'm surprised. You're not usually too perceptive with that sort of thing."

"Well, he's not doing much to hide it," I said.

"No, you're right," she said. "I hope it doesn't make you too uncomfortable, though. If you're okay with it,

I'm going to suggest Bubba set up roots in our city for a little while. I think having some friends around might help keep his addiction under control."

"I guess that makes . . . wait—what do you mean *our* city?" I asked. "I live there, but you only come in for business and the like. Isn't your actual apartment somewhere in the Midwest?"

"I wanted to make it a surprise, but I put in a transfer request, and it got accepted," Krystal said with a big grin. "The Agency is already looking for suitable apartments in your area."

"Really?" I said in shock. I knew things had been going well, but I'd never imagined she would go out of her way to be closer to me.

"Really," she assured me. "I'll still be gone a lot, of course. I have to go where the job takes me and all, but this means I don't have to keep making special trips. My default place in the world will be in the same town as you."

"And Albert," I reminded her.

"And your live-in zombie assistant," she said. "And Bubba, if his feelings don't make you feel too awkward."

I stopped to think about it. Yes, I was massively insecure that a girl like Krystal was with me, but her moving closer to me had given my confidence a shot of vigor. Aside from that, I knew what it was like to feel all alone in the world. Since I'd met Krystal, and even Albert, my life had felt far fuller than it ever had when I was alive.

Would it really be right of me to deny someone else that experience just because I had low self-esteem?

"Okay," I said, caving. "Tell him to get a place in Winslow. Just see if you can get him to not blatantly hit on you in front of me."

Krystal snorted out a laugh. "Hit on me? Freddy, Bubba is gay. Like really gay. Gayer than a unicorn butt-fucking a rainbow. You're the one he has a little crush on."

"What?"

"Yeah, you showed some real *huevos* today, and you saw how he stuck up for you a minute ago. I think you may have wooed him with your manly determination," Krystal said, barely suppressing her mirth at my misunderstanding.

"Oh . . . ohhh," I said. "Well, that makes it easier. Invite him out then."

"You're sure?"

"Positive," I said. "Let's get him away from this town of gambling and sin."

"Agreed," Krystal said with a smile. "I did have another question for you, though. What were you going to do if the challenge had been a chess match?"

"Win, of course," I told her. "I'm not sure if you remember, but I was quite the chess prodigy in high school."

Krystal reached over lovingly . . . and smacked me across my head.

"Ow!" I yelped in reflex. "What was that for?"

"I'm not sure if you remember, *Freddy*, but I was the only person you never managed to beat all through high school," Krystal reminded me. "So if I didn't beat their guy, what shot did you think you had?"

"I . . . might have forgotten that little detail."

"Thank god you're good-looking," Krystal said, giving me a half-hearted smile.

"You think so?"

"Nope, but you are my champion today, so shut up and give me a kiss while the boys are distracted with hot fudge."

All things considered, I'd had much worse Thanksgivings.

A MAGE AT THE PARK

1.

"PERIODONTIST," I SAID, CAREFULLY PLACING the tiles in position. "Thirty-six points."

The larger of my opponents surveyed the board, eyes darting about in the shadow of his ever-present ball cap, carefully examining his options. The man cut an intimidating figure, standing well over six-foot-six and sporting a physique that years of loading trucks had honed. Indeed, he would have been quite the adversary on another field of battle, but in this coliseum, muscles counted for nothing. He delved into his own supply of letters and made his play, his large fingers moving with surprising grace as he shuffled the new letters into position.

"Beer," said Bubba, leaning back in his chair. "Seven points."

"Good play!" Albert cheered.

"Go with what you know," Bubba said, picking up a fresh silver can and cracking it open.

I sighed inwardly and took a sip of my own drink, a glass of freshly decanted pinot noir. It was a bottle that had cost more than my usual range; however, things had been going quite well for my business as of late, so I felt it was a justified splurge. My guests had palates that were lower maintenance than my own: Bubba was drinking beer that came for ten dollars a case, and Albert was gulping down soda. Albert had only been seventeen when he died, so his tastes still ran to the adolescent. Of course, he'd also only been dead for a few months, and thus he hadn't had much time to mature his beverage preferences yet. Ah, but I should explain.

It turns out (as I'd already learned) that admittance into the club of ultra-powerful undead beings is much like buying a fantastic new home-theater system. Once the novelty wears off, you find yourself realizing that while the method of presenting it has greatly improved, the content generated is still just as lackluster as it was previously. In the same way that my robust flat screen is still shackled to showing reality TV and poorly-thought-out game shows, being a vampire doesn't particularly make me more interesting. If nothing else, though, it is proving to expand my social circle, and for that I am grateful.

"Albert, you're up," I said, prodding my assistant to make his move. He leaned across the table and stared at the board, tongue poking out ever so slightly in his fevered, yet cold-as-earth, concentration. Albert was an interesting fellow, easily the most upbeat person I'd ever met, both during my life and in the vampiric-after. Krystal had explained to me once that zombies were locked into the physiological state they'd been in at death, and it seems Albert had been . . . midway through . . . . Well, let us just say he was in an excellent frame of mind.

"Pony," Albert said, placing his tiles and sitting back into his chair.

Bubba cast a sidelong glance at the youthful undead; he could be a bit touchy about his size. However, nothing in Albert's chipper face betrayed a malicious intent, so Bubba shrugged his massive shoulders and refocused his attention on the beer. My own attention was settling back on the board, a bevy of tactical possibilities unfolding in my mind, when I heard footsteps thumping down the hallway outside my apartment. It took a few more seconds for the others to notice, as their hearing was not quite on par with mine.

"Sounds like someone is in a hurry," Bubba noted.

"Indeed," I said. "If not for Krystal's absence, I would find myself fearful that it was a troubled parahuman out looking for—"

"Help!" The cry was followed by an immediate rapping on my recently fortified door. Once upon a time, I had contented myself with the level of security provided by my apartment. However, the past few months had reminded me all too well that there was no such thing as too much precaution.

"Sir," I called cautiously. "I believe you have the wrong apartment."

"Albert! Please. Open up! I need your help!" And suddenly the whiny, pubescent tones of my unrequested visitor slipped comfortably into place among my memories.

"Oh, you must be joking." I sighed, walking over to the door and undoing the deadbolts before my assistant could beat me to it. I pulled back the heavy door to reveal another youthful face, though this one was aged a wee bit more than Albert's. It was bespectacled like my own, but leaner, with sandy brown hair that was sopping wet. The slightly freckled face was streaked with what looked like tears, and he was breathing raggedly, scarcely able to gulp the air down fast enough.

"Neil? Are you all right?" I asked.

"I'm fine," Neil spat out. "I need Krystal, though. I have to talk with her right now."

"Krystal is out of town," Bubba tossed in, his large eyes clearly curious about the visitor.

"She left for work," I said. "We don't know if she's in the state, or even the country."

"No, no, no, no, FUCK!" Neil smashed his small hand against my door. To put it simply, the door won.

"GAH!" I yelped, a bit overtaken by his sudden display of emotion. "What's wrong? Why do you need Krystal? Are you hurt? Can we help?"

"It's not me," Neil said, the tears making a renewed entrance to his pupils. "It's my mentor. She's missing, and her place is a wreck. I think someone kidnapped Amy."

"Ah. Well, then yes, I suppose that would be more a task for Krystal," I admitted.

A small whimper escaped from deep within Neil's throat.

"Fred," Albert said from the table. "We should try to help him. He's my best friend."

I took a mental tally. Neil had tried to overtake my girlfriend's mind, murder some innocent (if rather annoying) people, and had magically bound me in place for the better part of a night. But . . . he was Albert's best friend, and while I hadn't been blessed with an abundance of experience in the world of friendship prior to my death, I did understand the principles it entailed. Since I considered Albert something of a friend as well as an employee, I had to assume the transitive property was in place. I cared about Albert, Albert cared about Neil, so therefore, I cared about Neil as well.

Curses.

"Right. Well, you should at least come in and rest for a few minutes," I said, stepping aside to allow him entrance. "You can tell us what happened, and then we'll figure out if there is anything we can do."

In retrospect, that was the first of many mistakes.

2.

"LET'S TAKE IT FROM THE TOP," BUBBA SAID.

Neil nodded and took a sip of his water. He'd been sitting on my couch, chugging glass after glass for around five minutes. He still looked haggard, clothes stained with sweat and messenger bag tossed unceremoniously on the ground. He also looked less Goth than the last time I'd seen him, clothed more in pastels and muted browns, with the exception of an onyx collar around his neck. It didn't go with the rest of his ensemble, but I suppose change doesn't happen overnight. One could consider me an excellent example of that very point.

"I showed up at her place tonight, at six," Neil said, a hair of shakiness tickling his tone. "I go there every night for tutoring. Amy didn't answer when I banged on the door, though that's not so out of the ordinary—sometimes she gets caught up in her work. Anyway, I went around to the back door she usually leaves open."

Neil took another gulp of water and swallowed harder than it could have possibly required. "The place was wrecked. Beakers and glasses knocked on the floor, tables overturned, just a general sense of catastrophe. I searched for her all through the house, yelling out her name, but I got nothing in response."

"That sounds really scary." Albert rested a hand on his friend's shoulder in support.

"It was," Neil said. "And it got scarier the longer I couldn't find her. I didn't know what to do. I can't exactly call the cops to come snoop around a mage's home; God only knows what they might set off. But then I remembered the girl that arrested me that night, and how Albert said she hung out in Fred's apartment a lot of the time. It was the only thing I could think of, so I ran over here as fast as I could."

"You looked pretty wiped," I said.

"It was seven miles," Neil informed me. "And I've never been much of an athlete."

"I feel your pain there," I said. Living-Fred had been far from what one might be inclined to describe as graceful.

"Yeah, normally I'd make a snarky comment about vampires and cardio, but honestly, right now, I'm just hoping you guys can do something," Neil said.

"Look, Neil, I'm sorry about your mentor, but Krystal isn't here," I said, choosing my words carefully. The kid might have been all kinds of worked up and strung out. However, he was still a necromancer, and I was still a vampire. That's not the type of dynamic where you go pissing off the guy with magical powers. "She's the one with the training and experience at this sort of thing. I'm just an accountant."

"You aren't just an accountant," Neil snapped. "You're a vampire. Your kind is supposed to be crazy powerful. There has to be something you can do."

"I don't know. I mean, I guess *maybe* I could try to get her scent or something. I'll be honest, though, I played around with that back when I first got turned, and I'm not terribly good at it," I said. "Isn't there some sort of tracking magic you could do?"

"Sure I could, if I had access to my powers," Neil said, his eyes dropping toward the ground.

"What's stopping you?" Bubba said.

In response, Neil pointed to the black collar around his neck. "It's part of my probation. The collar binds my power unless I'm within twenty feet of my mentor, who is outfitted with a matching bracelet that acts as a key. Without Amy around, I'm just a normal human."

"That sucks," Albert quipped, summarizing the situation nicely in my opinion.

"Royally," Bubba chimed in.

"Indeed," I agreed.

"Yes, it blows goats, but that's not really the point right now," Neil said, pulling himself up from the couch. "What matters is that Amy is out there, in danger, and probably terrified."

"We understand. However, the fact remains that you're consulting with people who are ill prepared to assist in the job at hand," I said.

"I get that you guys don't know any more than me," Neil said. "But you've at least got some abilities. And you're the only people I can turn to with this. No matter what, I'm leaving here and trying to find Amy. I'll probably fail on my own, though. So, please, I need you to help her."

I wanted to protest our lack of suitability once more, but something in his words stuck out to me. Neil said he needed us to help *her*. He was specifically asking for assistance for another person's well-being. Mere weeks ago, he'd been willing to toss aside human lives for the chance at attaining greater power, yet now, here he was, unwavering in the need to save someone that was not himself. Whoever this Amy was, she must be quite the positive influence.

"I might know someone who can help," Bubba said, his thick drawl stretching out his words.

"Really?" Neil said. His eyes lit up with renewed hope.

"No promises," Bubba warned. "I can't guarantee he'll lend us any sort of a hand. If he does, though, we might have a genuine shot at finding your girl."

"A long shot is better than no shot," Neil said, scooping up his bag and walking to the door. "Let's go."

"We'll need something that belongs to her, something thick with her scent," Bubba informed him.

Neil patted his bag. "I thought that might be the case. I brought one of her spell books, a couple of scarves, and her favorite pipe."

"Then go outside to Fred's car and wait while we get our stuff," Bubba said. "Albert, you go keep him company."

"Aye, aye," Albert said, bounding over to his friend and exiting the apartment with him.

"What do we need to get?" I said, once the other two had left.

"Mentally prepared, because we might be stepping into a world of shit," Bubba said, setting down his beer. I could hear from the sloshing that it was only half finished, yet Bubba was abandoning it, his drinking clearly done. That, more than his tone, told me just how serious he was.

"Oh dear. I take it you're on less-than-stellar terms with this acquaintance?"

"It's not that. It's just that we're about to walk into the home of some serious heavy hitters in the parahuman world," Bubba said. "I'm hoping everything turns up roses. That said, if things start going south, you should be aware that we'll be in real trouble."

"You know, I think the three of you can handle this," I said hastily. "I don't see that I'll be able to contribute much at all."

Bubba laughed and slugged my shoulder. If not for my considerable undead augmentations, it would have doubtlessly sent me sprawling across the floor.

"That's the way to stay calm. Just keep joking," Bubba said.

"I'm not so much joking as you might hope. I'm pretty awful at this type of dangerous-situation, life-on-the-line sort of stuff."

"Nah," Bubba said, waving me off. "I thought that at first too, but after Vegas, I know you're a guy who comes through in a clutch. Just keep a level head, and we'll walk out of this fine."

As I was forcibly marched out my own door, scarcely giving me time to secure the locks, it occurred to me that perhaps my previous fever of momentary bravery had set an unrealistic standard in my companion's eyes. That wouldn't normally be so bad, but given my history of caving to peer pressure and the expectations of others, it could prove to be problematic.

3.

"ARE YOU SURE WE'RE IN THE RIGHT PLACE?" I yelled into Bubba's ear. I was yelling because we were in a nightclub in the posh section of downtown Winslow, with the noise so loud it was nearly impossible to hear anything else. Having enhanced senses has often been a boon to me since my change. But as the (and I'm being generous with this term) "music" pulsed with such vigor that it vibrated into my bones, I became keenly aware of the extent to which I missed my crappy mortal hearing.

Rather than imitate my shouting technique, Bubba merely nodded and gestured toward a set of elevators in the back of the building. We traversed a terrain thick with gyrating bodies, slowly inching our way closer to steel-doored salvation.

As we made our way through the crowd, it was quite apparent we stood out—and not in a positive way. These people were dressed in designer clothes, buying rounds of shots at a place where the beers cost fifteen dollars. In contrast, Bubba was wearing a flannel shirt and jeans; I was adorned in my usual button-down shirt, sweater-vest, and slacks; and Albert and Neil were both rocking an ensemble that would be considered casual even in high school. Factor in Bubba's exceptional height and the youth of the boys, and we should have been drawing a veritable abundance of sideways looks. And yet . . . no one was giving us a second glance. Their disinterest in our absurdity left me feeling all the more uncomfortable.

At last we reached the elevators, only to be immediately stopped by two muscular men in identical black suits. Bubba began what I can only describe as a game of high-stakes charades, trying to communicate to them some concept that I was unable to glean. Fortunately, the doormen were either more skilled or better informed than me, because, after some furtive gestures of their own, they stepped back. Bubba strode forward, and we followed suit. Once the elevator doors whispered shut, the blaring sound was almost completely silenced.

"Wow," I said. "That is some impressive sound insulation."

"Only the top of the line at this place," Bubba said. He punched the button for the highest floor, and the world jerked briefly as we ascended.

"Is that what all clubs are like?" Albert's eyes were wide; the sight had clearly left him a bit overwhelmed.

"No," I said. "Normally, the drinks are less expensive and the décor less tasteful. Also generally quieter, though that part can be variable." In truth, my experiences with clubs listed out to a total of two, though now, I supposed I could count it as three. I'd been dragged out twice during my time at college, and neither had ended particularly well. Please be aware that I would have happily considered being safely home in my bed as ending well, so that should give you some scope on just how poorly the evenings had gone.

"I'm more of a bar man myself," Bubba said. "Get me a nice beer and watch the game, maybe have some conversation. These damn places are too loud. You can't even hear yourself drink."

"Which begs the question, why are we here?" Neil said. "You said you knew somcone who would help."

"I said I knew someone who *could* help. Big difference there. And we're here because this is where he lives. The club is only the first floor of the building. Higher-up ones are offices for certain persons engaged in often less than legal activities."

"And we're going to the top," I said.

"Yup, because this guy is the worst kind of criminal," Bubba said.

"Smuggler?" Albert asked.

"Gun-runner?" Neil ventured.

"Assassin?" I guessed.

Bubba shook his head. "Politician."

We "*oooohed*" collectively as a group as understanding set in.

"What sort of politician would set up in a building with this reputation?" I wondered aloud.

"One whose mere existence is a matter of national secrecy. We're here to see the head of the therians in this area."

"I see. And therians are?"

"Shape-shifters," Bubba said. "It comes from 'therianthropy,' which is the term for everyone who turns into animals. There are way more of us than just wolves."

"So, this man presides over all of you?" I said.

"Sort of. It's mostly a position of honor. I had to come make nice with him when I moved to town—sign a few forms, initial a few boxes sayin' I wouldn't reveal myself or act like an asshole, that sorta thing. I know he also deals with other bureaucratic issues when they come up , though. So I guess you could think of him as a weremayor," Bubba said.

Albert chuckled. "That rhymes."

Despite the dire situation, I felt a brief, unbidden smile rise to my face. Only Albert could take joy in the sparse rhyming of "were" and "mayor" under such circumstance, but it was impossible not to take joy in Albert.

A loud ding informed us we had arrived at our destination. The doors slid open to reveal a white marble hallway leading forward. Immediately outside were another set of guards, though this set made the other pale in comparison. If the men we'd met when entering the elevator looked as if they could handle trouble, these men looked as though trouble would be sleeping with the light on for a week and double bolting its doors after even a brief encounter with them. They scanned us as we stepped out, assessing our overall threat level and presumably coming to the conclusion that we were acceptable. I had a feeling that that process only had one other potential outcome, and it was one I was quite thankful I wasn't experiencing.

We tread slowly across the plush red carpet, moving steadily forward. There were a set of steps some feet ahead that made it impossible to see what lurked at the end of the hallway, so instead, I contented myself with observing the tapestries hung along the walls. They showed a variety of man/animal hybrids in different historical scenes. One showed a creature I took to be a werebear wearing a Viking helmet and driving back a battalion of human warriors. Another seemed to feature a werewolf donned in armor kneeling before a king, the king's blade on the werewolf's shoulder as he bestowed knighthood. The last one before the beginning of the steps almost caused me to stumble, as it featured a wererat dressed in a crisp business suit with the White House in the background. I opened my mouth to ask Bubba about that one, but then decided perhaps it was better pursued after the business at hand was dealt with.

We crested the top of the stairs some seconds later, a whole new view meeting our eyes. What stood before us was a large room, the marble floor utterly covered in faux-fur rugs. A myriad of people lay on these rugs, some in various states of transformation. They looked on us hungrily as we walked into their line of sight, eyes unwavering from our all too fleshy forms. It was because of their aggression that they drew attention first. That is the only explanation I can give as to why I noticed them before the man sitting in their center.

I've previously described Bubba as one of the largest men I'd ever met, and while that description was apt at the time, seeing this man rendered it invalid. Seven feet tall and certainly several feet wide, this man was the thing NFL scouts' wildest fantasies are made of. His entire humongous body was carved muscle. Golden hair, wild and untamed, fell to his ludicrously broad shoulders. His teeth were just a few shades too white and far, far too many shades too sharp. He rested on a white throne of the same marble the hallway was constructed of. There were no rugs, faux-fur or otherwise, softening the seat for him. If it was uncomfortable (which I'm certain it had to have been), he banished any such indicators from his square-jawed face. His bright green eyes moved over us one at a time. When his gaze fell on me, I found myself profoundly grateful that I no longer needed to breathe, since hyperventilation was then not a possibility. When he finished scrutinizing us, he spoke, his voice rough as a law degree and deeper than Plato.

"Bubba Emerson. What brings you and your guests to my den tonight?"

"We come seeking aid for a mage who has gone missing," Bubba said, his words concise and his tone subdued.

"A mage? What do I care for the life of a mage? My duty is to the therians of this city. You know that."

Bubba nodded. "I do. However, I had hoped that you might be willin' to direct us to a therian with strong tracking skills, in the hopes of fostering good will. Besides, there are worse people to have owe you a favor than a mage."

The giant of a man sat silent for a few moments, pondering Bubba's appeal.

"No," he said at last. "If the mage has been taken, it is undoubtedly at someone else in our world's behest. I see no benefit in embroiling my people in such a potentially dangerous situation. I wish you the best, but I can provide no aid."

"I understand," Bubba said. "Thank you for hearin' our request." Bubba turned around and motioned for us to do the same. I turned readily, and Albert did with some reluctance.

Neil was having none of it though.

"You said he would help us," Neil whispered furtively.

"I said he *could* help us, and I tried hard to make you recognize the difference in the two. We got a 'no.' Now turn around, and leave," Bubba whispered right back.

"No . . . no, this can't be it," Neil said, shaking his head. Before Bubba could react, Neil darted to the side and dashed by him, moving closer to the weremayor. Instantly, there were growls from the rug ensemble, matched by tensed muscles ready to pounce. Neil seemed to notice none of this.

"Please! I'm begging you, sir. Please help us. My mentor is a good woman, kind and loving to everyone she meets. She's a great person in addition to being a great mage." Neil dropped to his knees and lowered his head. "I'm not asking for much. Just the name of someone who can track her. I'm begging you. Please, help Amy."

Bubba pulled the small adolescent up with one hand and firmly clamped the other over his mouth.

"I'm sorry 'bout my guest, sir," Bubba said, haste garbling his words slightly. "He's a whelp and hasn't learned better yet. I assure you, I'll instruct him of these lessons myself. We'll leave your den in peace now." Bubba turned around once more, but this time, the weremayor spoke before he could take a step.

"Wait. The boy said the mage was named Amy. Amy Wells?"

Neil nodded from his hoisted position above the ground.

"That changes things," the giant said. He pointed to a door near the rear of the room. "I will deal with you in my quarters."

Bubba swallowed hard, but complied with the order and began walking toward the door. Albert and I followed, though I direly wished the weremayor had chosen a term besides "deal with" to describe our impending interaction.

4.

THE MASSIVE DOOR—ALSO MARBLE—CLOSED behind us with an audible *thud*. The weremayor switched some sort mechanism to lock it in place, though, for the afterlife of me, I couldn't have told you why he bothered. The thing weighed several hundred pounds, so I'm not sure who could have possibly moved it besides him. (Well . . . me, I suppose. Perhaps Bubba, if he were transformed. Albert could probably have budged it too; zombies are surprisingly strong. And then, of course, if Neil had been in control of his magic, he almost certainly would have been capable. Actually, in light of the fact that everyone in the room could have moved the door, a locking mechanism makes much more sense than I realized in that moment.)

"Amy Wells," he growled, as he finished locking the door. "I'm very unhappy to hear that something has happened to her."

"With the services of a good tracker, we hope to recover her," Bubba said.

"I cannot merely *assign* you a tracker," the hulking man said down to us. "This situation is somewhat . . . complicated."

We all stood around quietly, uncertain of what to say next. Generally speaking, I'd learned over and over again not to pry into the life of someone stronger than you. Admittedly, that category had once consisted of a much larger percentage of the population, which might help explain my lackluster social skills; however, the principle was a sound one. The man stared each of us down, as though he were looking deep into our minds, past our souls, to where we hid our deepest fears . . . and he was taking notes.

At last, he let out a sigh. His shoulders appeared to sag a bit, and the tension in his neck relaxed. He was still an enormous, imposing man, yet somehow, a good portion of the fear he inspired seemed to diminish.

"Bubba Emerson," he said.

"Yes, Mr. Alderson?"

The weremayor waved him off. "Please, call me Richard. I think you and I will soon be on far more familiar terms. Bubba Emerson, the things I am about to tell you are not secrets, per se. But, that said, I do not relish the idea of them being freely discussed. Do you take my meaning?"

"Quite clearly." Bubba nodded.

"And the rest of you?"

"Implicitly," I replied.

"Clear as day," Neil said, with more confidence than he possibly could have felt.

"Yup!" The last one was Albert. I have a feeling you already figured that out though.

"Good, then here is what you need to know," Richard said. "Amy Wells is currently acting as a private tutor to a therian in my town. This therian is very special to me, so I do not take the abduction of her teacher lightly. I take it, in fact, as a personal insult."

Bubba let out a low-pitched whistle between his teeth. I didn't know much about therian society, but I could piece together that when a man Richard's size said "personal insult," the dilemma would likely end with someone spending a long time in a hospital contemplating the error of their ways.

"With that as the case, I will be personally assisting you in locating the mage," Richard concluded.

"That's great," Neil said, relief practically dripping out of him. "I've got the things you can use to track her right here."

"There is something I must attend to first. It will take some time, but I will be as quick as possible. I trust there are no objections?" Richard said, a tremor of growl slipping back into his voice.

We all nodded emphatically, quite possibly in perfect unison.

Rather than acknowledging us verbally, Richard strode across the room to another set of doors. The room itself was quite impressive: oversized furniture for someone of his mass; lush, ankle-deep carpets; paintings hung across the walls; and a roaring fireplace easily big enough to roast a pig in. When Richard reached the room's edge, he threw open the double doors and revealed to us yet another space.

This one was painted pink, with small bits of furniture all over the place. Drawings hung on the wall rather than majestic, framed artworks, and the pink, carpeted floor was littered with craft supplies. This room also held two new people in it—a small boy and girl. Upon seeing the doors open, the girl leapt from her position coloring on the floor and dashed toward our host.

"Daddy!" she squealed, as Richard scooped her up in one of his massive arms. He set her on his shoulder, where she immediately entwined her hands in his hair to give herself a safe grip. She couldn't have been more than five or six, with golden locks the same as her father's and tied off in a pair of pigtails. Her voice was high and squeaky, peppered with levels of enthusiasm attainable only by children and drug addicts.

"You finished early today!"

"Not exactly, Sally," Richard said. "Daddy still has some work to do tonight."

"Awwww," Sally moaned, pulling on his hair. "You always have to work late. You said tonight would be early. You promised."

"I did not promise." Richard sighed. "I said I would try my best."

"Same thing."

Richard cast us a quick glance and shrugged as if to say, "Kids."

"Sally, Daddy has to do a favor for Miss Amy tonight." Richard delicately plucked her from the perch on his shoulder. It looked like the endeavor wound up costing him about two five-year-old fist-sized portions of his hair, but he bore it with nary a grimace.

"Miss Amy is coming? Yaaaaaaay!" Sally began running around in circles, waving her hands like she was certain the secret to flying was just in how hard she flapped.

"No, Sally, Miss Amy needs Daddy's help with something. That's why he has to work late. Daddy has to go out to her."

"Oh." Sally's disappointment could not have been more palpable. It's curious that children can either be expert liars or utterly incapable of hiding their emotions, and the classification changes from minute to minute.

"I guess if it's for Miss Amy, then it's okay," Sally relented after a few moments. "But tomorrow, I want to have dinner with Daddy."

"Daddy will try his best," Richard said. "Now, if you go wash up, Daddy can tuck you into bed before he goes."

"Okay!" Sally cried, dashing off into a connected room and slamming the door behind her.

"Sorry," Richard said as he turned to us, though I had no idea precisely what he was apologizing for. "She's at that age."

There was a derisive snort, and for a moment, I was confused. It hadn't come from one of us, and it hadn't come from Richard. The girl was out of the room, so who was left? That's when I once again noticed the other child in the room. He'd been sitting at the same plastic table, quietly coloring during Richard and Sally's entire exchange. The boy's skin was so tan it bordered on copper. His hair was an inky black. Noticing him for the second time, I couldn't shake the feeling that there was something . . . off in the way he moved. Nothing I could pin down, just something . . . different.

"Did you have a comment, Gideon?" Richard asked the young boy, whose attention seemed to be fully occupied by the act of coloring.

"Just that I happen to like you people best at 'that age.'" Gideon didn't even bother to stop coloring as he responded. I blinked in surprise. His voice didn't fit with his form. Physically, he couldn't have been a day over seven, and was likely closer to Sally in age. His voice was strong, though, strong and mature. No, more than mature—old. And I mean "old" not in the way of denture cream and dinner at four. "Old" in the way of mountains.

"I suppose I can see the appeal," Richard said, his eyes darting to the door Sally had sealed herself behind. A gentle smile, one I could never have imagined ten minutes ago, crested his chiseled face for a moment.

After that, we were blessed with a brief bit of silence, until the door flung open and Sally's voice thundered forth from its interior.

"Daddy! Come read me a story and tuck me in!"

"If you gentlemen will excuse me, we can leave as soon as I'm done," Richard said, heading toward the door. He paused as he passed the young boy. "Gideon, these people are my guests. Please treat them as such."

"Yes, yes, laws of hospitality and such. Nothing to worry about," Gideon replied, without glancing up from his paper. With that reassurance, Richard went into the other room and shut the door.

The four of us looked at each other at first, no one entirely sure what was going on or what to say about the situation. A few of us threw glances at the boy, Gideon, but it seemed I wasn't the only one who was a little spooked by him. Our eyes dashed over his diminutive form, curious to get a better look, yet terrified of being caught. Finally, it was the boy who broke the silence. In retrospect, he might have been the only one who could have.

"So, something happened to Mage Wells," Gideon said, setting down his crayons and standing from the small chair he'd been resting in. "I find that unfortunate."

"Did she teach you too?" Albert asked.

Gideon snickered. "Other way around, deadling. Sally is very fond of her, though, and I am always displeased to see Sally sad."

He began walking toward us, a simple endeavor, and yet it made me feel like I had swallowed a brick. I shook my head and tried to get control of myself. I had never been a particularly brave person; however, fighting the urge to cower in front of a child was a step beyond even my usual levels of conflict aversion.

Bubba and Albert squirmed uncomfortably next to me. In fact, Neil was the only one who seemed to be blissfully unaware of the aura being generated by this dark-haired child.

"A therian, a deadling, a bound mage, and a blood-eater. Not exactly the rescue party I would put together in this situation," Gideon said.

"Me either." The words slipped out of my mouth before the overall feeling of dread could warp or silence them. Gideon smiled at that, and as he came within a few feet of us, he raised his eyes for the first time, gazing into mine. In that moment, I understood why I'd been so uncomfortable since I first noticed him.

The funny thing about becoming a vampire is how little things seemed to change for me. My weight, sure, and of course the physical boons were readily apparent. The downsides (silver, sunlight allergies, etc.) were also pretty obvious. The mental aspect, though, that was more subversive. It manifested on some primal, subconscious level, and it had taken me a while to realize that I now regarded everyone around me as prey. I made peace with it early on, though, and had rarely spared a thought about the subject since. But I should have, because when I looked into Gideon's purple eyes, my brain slammed me with the realization that my mind had been too stupid to comprehend. Prey wasn't the only thing that existed in the world around me.

There were also predators.

5.

BY THE TIME WE GOT TO AMY'S OFFICE, I'd mostly recovered from my scare, though I was still a bit shaken. Thankfully, the raging impulse to run and hide (and pray to whatever god happened to care about accountants) had mostly diminished. It was still a bit embarrassing that I'd cowered in the corner while the rest of the team waited for Richard, but given what he told us when we piled into Bubba's extra-large truck, I felt at least somewhat justified in my primal-brain powered cowardice.

"A dragon," I said, for what was approximately the seventeenth time. "How do we have a dragon in our city? I mean, it seems like someone would have noticed."

"Gideon likes to keep a low profile," Richard explained, fidgeting as he tried to get comfortable. Despite the extended cab on Bubba's truck, the two robust men had little space to move, especially with me, Albert, and Neil crammed in as well. "Dragons have a vast amount of magic. Taking the form of a lesser being is easy for them."

"Can he turn into a dog?" Albert asked, his eyes sparkling as untold shape-shifting possibilities danced through his head. Whatever panic mechanism Gideon had triggered in my brain, it clearly wasn't installed in zombies.

"He can turn into almost anything," Richard said. "But he usually stays in that form."

"A child seems like a curious choice for a powerful dragon." Much as Gideon terrified me, I couldn't quite resist the urge to understand more about him.

Something flickered across Richard's face, an emotion between guilt and uncertainty. I wasn't so stupid as to dig further. Whatever he was feeling, it obviously didn't engender a desire to chat. Regardless, it was at precisely that moment that Bubba swerved into a driveway and killed the engine. We had arrived at Amy's abode.

She lived in a reasonably-sized house surrounded by ample foliage. There was more greenery on her property than in the entire square mile around my apartment.

We were only a few blocks outside of downtown, too, so whatever Amy did to pay the bills, she must have been good at it. Lots this size, in this area, were far from cheap. A fact that was echoed in the placement of the other houses—nearby, but none too close to hers.

"Her lab is in back," Neil said, darting out of the truck and speed-walking around the side of the building. Albert kept up with him, though barely. Bubba and Richard took their time extricating themselves from the vehicle. The caution was understandable. With their size and strength, it would be all too easy to bend a door or break a window. Eventually they got free, and we followed Neil to a large wooden door in the back of the house. There were symbols scrawled all over it. They might have been magical; then again, they might have been Japanese, for all I knew. I was about to step through when it occurred to me that a mage might have security features in place that were far more effective than just a deadbolt. None of the others seemed worried about it, though, and since they walked past and didn't seem to disintegrate, I followed.

I hadn't known what a mage's laboratory would be like, but the one thing I didn't expect was an actual, well . . . laboratory. Beakers, tubing, microscopes, three computers, a bevy of plants, and shelves of materials greeted me upon entrance. Not literally though. Animated tools—that, I actually would have expected. Instead,

I got a sterile environment that looked more like it belonged to a botanist than someone who dabbled in the arcane arts. Though, the fact that about a quarter of it was wrecked or broken did somewhat dilute the effect.

"Shit," Richard growled from the other side of the room. He was hunkered into a squat, looking at a pile of broken glass and burned book pages. There were scorch marks on the table next to him, as well as a half-melted, cylindrical beaker. I took a breath in surprise, and a very familiar scent caught my attention. It was something I could have picked out of a thousand, one my brain was unfortunately programmed to prioritize above all other things.

Blood. There was blood on the table. I moved over slowly and took a closer look. It was smeared across the corner, a solid swipe about three inches long by two inches wide.

"Looks like the kid was right," Richard said. "There was a struggle."

"The blood is fresh. No more than four hours old." I spoke before I even realized the objective strangeness of such a statement, but fortunately, none of the others were bothered by my blood-assessing abilities.

"Neil arrived at Fred's place around two hours ago," Bubba said. "So, whatever happened, it probably happened half an hour before six."

"Why does it matter what time it happened?" Neil shuffled lightly as he spoke, eyes darting around the room with a frantic energy.

"It matters because Amy is not some powerless human," Richard snapped. "She is a mage with significant skills and a wealth of experience. There is only a small list of things I can think of that could break into a mage's lab, abduct her, and not leave behind a few pounds of flesh in the process. Knowing it happened at five-thirty tells us it was just after dusk, which expands that list. Whatever took her is powerful, and we'd better hope we figure out what it was before we catch up to them."

"Oh." Neil lowered his head and slunk quietly back over to Albert.

"I've got her scent," Richard continued. "Fred, what about you?"

"I think so. What do we do now?"

"We follow it."

Our group went back to the truck, but when I went to climb in, I felt a massive hand close around my shoulder.

"We're in the back," Richard informed me. I hopped into the bed of the truck, then scrambled out a few seconds later when Richard bounded over the side and nearly landed on top of me. The truck dipped down under his weight, losing several inches before rebounding most of the way back up. I climbed back in and found some space near the tailgate while the others entered the front. Bubba turned the keys, and the engine barked harshly to life. Richard pounded once on the roof and pointed south, further down the street we'd traveled to get here. I sniffed experimentally and found that I could still pick out the scent of Amy's blood in the air.

"Thank you for doing this, by the way," I said, raising my voice over the unmuffled engine sounds and the wind blowing past us. "I didn't get to say it back at your club."

"Sally does not have the easiest life. My position makes great demands on my time, and I must leave her alone far more than I would like. Amy is not just a teacher to Sally—she is a friend. She adds a level of familiarity and happiness to my daughter's life. That is not something I care to see taken away from her. The one who owes thanks is me, for bringing her dilemma to my attention."

"I think that credit goes to Neil. He's the one who's been screaming his head off until someone would listen."

Richard slapped the roof again and yelled "Left!" so loudly that I imagine everyone in the neighborhood suddenly turned that direction in their sleep. He turned back to me as Bubba yanked the wheel and sent us onto a worn, blacktop road. "Yes, her apprentice is very loyal. Not that I'm terribly surprised. Amy has a way with people."

"Sounds like it." I drew in some air and confirmed I could still smell her. I probably could have found out where she went by veering around to see when I could and couldn't smell her, but I had no idea how Richard was able to pin down her direction so effortlessly. It could have been that his sense of smell was that much stronger than mine, or it could have been that he'd practiced this. I had never really been chomping at the bit to expand my vampire repertoire, though, since meeting Krystal, my horizons were definitely widening.

"I'll introduce you, when we recover her," Richard said. He lapsed into silence, save for the occasional thud on the hood and hollered direction. I wondered if Bubba would need the number of a good mechanic to buff out the dents in his roof, then realized Bubba was the kind of person who was perfectly capable of fixing that himself. We were nearing the heart of the suburban community—a large park that was partially obscured by trees. I could make out a winding sidewalk that seemed to wrap around the edge as well as branching off toward the center.

We passed a gazebo situated on a small lake, and it hit me: Amy's smell was stronger here. Much stronger. Evidently, Richard reached the same conclusion, because he yelled for Bubba to find a parking spot. The truck lurched around, eventually coming to the park entrance, where a small, wooden sign informed visitors that it was closed for the day. It was the kind of sign used in neighborhoods full of nice, law-abiding people who have great respect for the rules. It shattered to splinters as Bubba drove over it.

"We could have just moved it," I said to no one in particular.

"Therian Emerson is a good man, but not the most delicate."

"You can say that again." The truck shuddered to a stop, and I hopped out, eager to put a little distance between me and Richard before he exited. The others were still in the truck, so I headed forward and tested my nose's abilities. I stepped onto the grass, my loafers immediately growing damp. The scent was less intense than it had been in her laboratory. Probably because, by the time she got here, the cut had stopped bleeding. I could still find her scent, but it was duller, muted. The damn thing was everywhere, though. If she wasn't in this park, she had been very recently.

I had turned back to relay my findings to the others when I felt something wrap around my leg with incredible speed. There was a rustling sound, a snap of motion, and suddenly I found myself being hauled further away from the parking lot. I flipped over on my back and found my abductor was a long, leafy vine. Breaking it should have been no problem. The issue at hand was that I couldn't bend forward far enough to reach it. Inwardly cursing myself for not sticking to my morning stretches, I clawed uselessly at the ground, tearing out chunks of wet sod, but not visibly slowing down.

When I was able to glance back, I saw the others hadn't noticed my kidnapping yet. I opened my mouth to yell for them; however, that was when the vine stopped pulling me on the ground and lifted me into the air. I twirled about, spinning helplessly as I rose. I was very thankful that vampires couldn't throw up. What I was somewhat less thankful for was that my shifting view treated me to the occasional look at what the vine was connected to.

The creature was twenty feet tall and resembled a pile of moss with vines and branches sticking out. It had no discernible eyes or face. In fact, the only thing it *did* have, aside from foliage, was a mouth. Oh, and teeth. A giant mouth with rows and rows of what looked like very sharp teeth. I know this because, as I was dangling in its grasp, that mouth was opening wider and wider. With those contextual clues, even Albert could have figured out what was going to happen next in this process. Now was clearly the time for action, so I resolved myself to do what I did best.

"HEEEEEEELP! SOMEBODY HELP ME!"

6.

FUN PHYSIOLOGY FACT: THE HUMAN BODY is wired to respond with a cacophony of terror when it hears certain sounds. This is a leftover of our hunter days, when the people who didn't have such instincts wound up dead. And, as it turned out, some of those responses are wired so deep that not even undeath can purge them. This is why, as scared as I was of the moss monster intent on turning me into an *amuse-bouche*, the tremendous roar of an approaching lion cranked my fear levels up to where I was too frozen to even scream. I thought I was as terrified as I could possibly be . . . and then I saw the beast that had made the noise.

This king of the jungle was massive. It was easily bigger than a horse, and I'm not talking about one Bubba's size. Its huge muscles propelled it forward with astonishing speed. The extra size did nothing to diminish its graceful movements as it leapt from the ground and sank tremendous fangs into the moss monster, or "mosster," as I would later deem it. The creature let out a wheezing moan. Whatever force of the universe had created it had evidently forgotten to put in a tongue or vocal chords. The mosster turned its attention on the several hundred pounds of slashing-and-biting lion that was screwing up its dinner plans.

Not one to waste an opportunity to run away, I swung myself upward and snatched at the vine holding me. It took a few tries before I finally got my hand around the leafy appendage. After that, the rest was easy. Vampire strength might not let me lift cars, but I will tear up some shrubbery all day long. My landing was far from graceful. Cats might always land on their feet. However, the same cannot be said for accountants. After a quick scramble up from the ground, I checked on the status of my savior.

The lion had carved away large swaths of the mosster's outer layer, exposing a sort of tree-root skeleton beneath. Now, for a real lion, that would have been a challenge; people underestimate how dense a live branch can be. But this particular over-sized feline was far from normal, and its powerful jaws turned the skeleton into splinters as fast as it was revealed.

"Fred, you okay?" Bubba had jogged over while my attention was focused on the strange spectacle. Beneath the brim of his faded ball cap I could see a worried expression on his sizable face. "That thing didn't get a piece of you, did it?"

"No, thankfully the giant lion managed to intervene before I found out if vampires can survive digestion." We both then turned to watch the battle. Even in the strange parahuman world that we occupied, it was still an odd and captivating show.

"Impressive, isn't he?"

"That's definitely a word. So, unless Neil or Albert learned some new tricks, I'm guessing that's Richard?"

Bubba held up the shirt and pair of pants that had previously been on the weremayor. "Yup."

"Why is he so big? I know therians usually turn into larger forms of their animals, but . . . my goodness."

"Like all animals, you get some that are runts and some that are alpha-sized. Richard is one of the biggest around. It's part of why he can stand over the therian community. We tend to respect people who can kick our asses."

Richard was definitely demonstrating that talent on the mosster. It had been reduced to little more than a flapping mouth and mulch. Even its vine tendrils had been unable to stop the lion's relentless assault. As he snapped through one of what could probably be called its legs, I noticed the edges of it were melting away. They smeared along the ground in tiny green rivers, vanishing after getting a few feet from the source.

Neil was the one who answered my evident look of curiosity, he and Albert finally catching up to the rest of us. Zombies can move quickly when they want to. Nerds who ran LARPs were generally less inclined toward cardiovascular exertion, though. Tugging at the collar around his neck and wiping sweat off his brow, Neil panted for a few moments before commenting on the dissolving mosster.

"Magic," he said, as though that was all the clarification that was required.

"Augmented construct, actually," Richard added. He'd shifted back to his human form so rapidly there hadn't even been time to register it. Bubba coughed with a deep rumble, turned his eyes purposefully toward the ground, and thrust out his hands with Richard's clothing. The rest of us followed suit, giving the man what privacy we could while he covered himself.

"Amy has taught Sally the basics of such magic. It revolves around creating a mindless servant from the materials at hand. Her lesson merely involved dancing paper figures, though." It didn't take long for him to slip back into his pants—it seemed like this was a situation he found himself in with some frequency—and he didn't even bother with the shirt, tucking it into his waistband and leaving his massive torso exposed to the chilly November air. To his credit, Bubba did an excellent job of not staring, despite Richard's objectively impressive physique. The man looked like a living statue from a civilization of oversized warriors. I didn't play for the same team as Bubba, and I was still struck with admiration.

"As much as I like knowing what that was, could someone tell me why it was here? Or better yet, why it decided to eat me?"

"Amy's scent is strong here. I think we can surmise that her abductor is another mage, one who thought to leave traps for anyone who might pursue them. As to its appetite, you were merely the first to get close. It was fortunate you did, though. Now we know to be on the lookout."

"Magical traps and monsters." I sighed. Not for the first time that night, I wished Krystal was there. Despite being the only human in our group (at least as far as I could tell), she was the best skilled for this sort of work. Wishing didn't make things happen, though, not unless genies were real—which reminds me actually, I should check into that. But, at any rate, she wasn't with us, and we still had a kidnapped mentor to find.

"Oh, and thank you for saving me. Almost forgot my manners in the craziness," I added after a moment.

Richard gave me a sideways glance that I was getting used to seeing from a lot of people. I got the feeling I didn't mesh too well with other people's expectations of vampires. That was fine. I didn't match what I'd expected either. "You are welcome. Amy's trail leads into the woods. Is everyone ready to pursue?"

"Hang on." Bubba shrugged off his denim jacket, removed his faded baseball hat, kicked off his boots, and stuffed them all into a backpack he'd brought along from the truck. He kept his gray T-shirt and worn jeans on. However, it was clear he wanted to be able to shift rapidly if required. I bit my tongue at suggesting he might be more effective in his human form. As I've already said, Bubba could be a little sensitive about his size. Besides, even if he wasn't as big as most weresteeds, he still packed a lot of kick into that little form.

Neil walked over while Bubba was stripping down and picked up a pair of sizable tree limbs that were left over from the mosster. Though most of the magical construct had dissolved (and thankfully the mouth was part of that), there was still a pile of grass clippings and branches. Rejoining us, Neil handed one of the limbs to Albert and let the other rest against his shoulder. It seemed everyone was getting ready for a throw down.

We darted into the nearest cluster of trees—Bubba right on Richard's (not literal) tail, Albert and I hanging back a bit with Neil. After a hundred yards, it became clear that the mage wouldn't be able to keep up with us on foot, which was fair, given that two of us had supernatural endurance, and two of us didn't have to breathe. So we paused while Albert allowed his friend to climb into piggy-back position. Our pace increased after that, leaving the first cluster of trees and coming out near the gazebo I'd seen from the road.

Richard turned and began following one of the sidewalks, dashing past the small lake and ducking under a lamppost. I wondered what a human observer would take us for if they saw our strange parade. Drug addicts seemed like a solid bet; stoners chasing some invisible target or running from some imagined beast. I missed the days when I would silently judge seemingly crazy people in a park, instead of being one of them.

We ran up a small hill toward another cluster of trees, but as we crested the top, Richard stopped short. It only took a few steps and a slight shift in perspective to see what had brought him up to a halt so quickly. Bustling about the border of the tree line were squat, semi-human-shaped creatures about three feet in height. Their color was somewhere between an eggshell and a pasty yellow. Squished faces with beady eyes sat atop their muscular bodies. The large caps on their heads made me think they seemed like pale midgets wearing sombreros.

"Heh, heh," Albert giggled. "Does anyone else think those look like . . . never mind."

"Dicks," Bubba said. "Like walking dicks that have been juicing. I guess that means they started off as mushrooms."

"Regardless of what they started as, I trust we all know where they are going." Richard said, bringing us back to the task at hand. Bubba started to pull off his shirt, but the weremayor held up a hand and stopped him. "I don't think there is any need for that. Half-form should be enough for these pests."

I'd learned at a very troublesome high school reunion that therians could be full human or full animal, but they also had a step in between. It's weaker than their full animal shape; however, it has the benefit of getting to hang on to things like opposable thumbs and the ability to speak.

Richard's change was so rapid that even watching him closely, I barely caught all the details. Golden hair sprouted around his neck and across his entire body, which somehow managed to add several inches in height and tens of pounds of muscle. His face flattened into a cat-like nose set just above a large mouth filled with teeth clearly meant for evisceration. Each of his fingernails elongated sharply, tapering off to a point that I had no doubt was sharp enough to cut flesh. Possibly bone.

Bubba's hybrid form was somewhat less impressive. Though he did grow wider and a touch thicker, he lost about a foot of height, putting him at eye level with the rest of us. His arms were longer than before, with a thick, shiny black surface running across the back of his hands along the knuckles. Dark brown fur about an inch long seemed to be growing out of every visible area except for his head, which had darkened to a near black. Facially, he looked like someone had run his face through a funhouse mirror, stretching it up and down like flesh taffy.

"You three, stay back," Richard growled, making Neil and me both leap off the ground in terror. (Remember what I said about sounds and genetic wiring? He had crossed that vocal threshold.) "This will go faster if we don't have to work around you."

Bubba snorted, though whether it was in agreement or derision, I had no idea. Richard clearly did, as he bounded down the hill toward his unsuspecting prey, a significantly smaller, but equally hairy form only a few steps behind him.

For my part, I crouched down into a squat and tried to get comfortable. It was going to be nice to finally see what winning an easy one looked like.

7.

"FASTER. FASTER. FASTER!" NEIL YELLED, clutching Albert's back in a death grip while swinging back on occasion to check the progress of our pursuers. I had no such need. My excellent hearing had become a curse, informing me of just how close the giant mushroom-men were. Of course, it may also have helped that their enormous feet made a truckload of noise with each step.

We'd discovered that not all constructs are simply made and then bound to their form. I would later learn that a particularly skilled mage can impart special properties to their creations, properties such as, for example, the ability to grow nine feet taller and proportionally larger when threatened. Of course, that alone would actually have not been an unassailable hurdle, not for Richard and Bubba anyway. No, what had taken them down was the other aspect these mushmen possessed. A sound like pudding being churned came from behind, and I dearly missed the time in my life several minutes ago when I didn't know what that meant.

"Incoming!" I risked a glance back as I yelled, trying to calculate which one was firing and where to dodge. Two of them had swollen cheeks and closed mouths, as though they were holding their breath. If only that were the truth. I veered left and saw Albert go right, both of us dodging the thick wads of acid that landed where we had been only seconds before. The goo covered a wide patch of ground, hissing and bubbling as it destroyed all it touched. Even the seemingly invincible Richard had looked pretty horrific after getting doused in it, right before he screamed at us to hightail it out of there. From Bubba I knew that, short of silver and beheading, there wasn't much a therian couldn't regenerate from. I was far less certain about the effects of acid on undead flesh, though, and I knew for certain it would dissolve Neil down to bone, hence our escape. In sheer panic, we ran into the very trees the mushmen had been guarding, since I thought their sudden growth spurt would hinder their pursuit. I'd been right, however not by nearly as much as I needed to be.

The dodge had kept us alive—well, in a manner of speaking—yet I could hear more churning pudding from behind me, so we were far from in the clear. There was another issue, as well; the wide splash zone had separated Albert and Neil from me. We were now running at a right angle, growing steadily further apart. I tried to alter my course, but the next volley of acid wads forced me to scramble in a zigzag line to keep from becoming a vampire-accountant puddle. If you're wondering how I was so adept at this, given my usual track record of efficiency, let me just say that while I am not skilled in many things, I am a twentieth-degree black belt in running away.

The mushmen had split up to follow both of us. I had two on my tail, which meant that wherever Albert was, he was running from three. I worked to push that thought out of my mind, not out of lack of concern, but rather because there was nothing I could do aside from trust him. Besides, I still had the pressing matter of my own adversaries barreling down on me. Vampire speed mixed with an inability to feel fatigue meant that there were very few things I couldn't outrun. However, their enormous size, stride, and similar endurance seemed to register these creatures in that very same category. The only blessing I had was that they took time between acid blasts, presumably meaning there was some sort of recharging process. I used the grace period to double down on my speed, pushing with all I had to place some distance between us.

The gap between the mushmen and me was widening slowly. I probably didn't have much time left before they could fire again. I leapt over a particularly large fallen log, misjudging its height and barely clearing the top, and landed in a sprint. I was already a few steps away when I heard something that was tremendously confusing. Silence. No great, crashing feet wrecking their way in pursuit of me. I risked a glance over my shoulder to see something truly surprising, and by this point in the night, that was not an easy bar to reach.

Both mushmen had stopped at the log. They were milling about, looking at me with what I would guess was either hate or frustration, though given the inhuman composition of their faces, that is obviously, as I said, a guess. What was certain was that they'd hit some sort of barrier. Each was careful to not even so much as brush against the log, keeping away from it with the same careful fear I'd shown in avoiding their acid. Eventually, they turned back and lumbered slowly away, twisting their heads around occasionally to see if I would leave my area of protection. They were in for quite a disappointment.

Without the focus-narrowing stimulation of eminent destruction, I found my mind wandering over what my next move should be. Bubba and Richard should be safe. With us leading the mushmen away, they would have had time to regenerate. Albert might still be getting chased. But if the constructs had one area limit, it stood to reason they had more. Perhaps the enchantments that sustained them were bound to a particular region. I was seemingly safe; however, that was likely a temporary status. We still had a kidnapper on the loose, skilled with magic and fond of setting traps. I couldn't very well go back, though. I knew the mushmen were beyond my ability to deal with. Maybe the next challenge would be something more my speed. Like a turtle, or a three-legged frog.

Walking away from my savior log, I realized that though it had seemed silent with the sudden ceasing of the mushmen's stomping, there was still a sound pricking at my ears. It was a strange combination of hoots, chirps, whistles, and brush rustling. And it was close.

Moving with as much care and silence as I could, I crept through the trees and over the shrubbery. The noise grew louder and, somehow, stranger. These weren't just random wilderness noises. There was a pattern to them, one that was somehow familiar and unfamiliar all at once. About a quarter of a mile from the log, the ground sloped down, creating a divot in the forest, like a grassy bowl. Sitting in the center of it was a woman in her mid-thirties, brown hair tied in a series of complicated braids that had come halfway out, and clothed in a flowing dress that had been stained with grass and mud. She sat on a rock, swaying quietly as the various animals and plants around her continued their odd serenade. Her eyes were open, but I had no idea what their natural color was, because, instead of a visible iris or pupil, a rainbow of shifting colors moved along her eyeball, obscuring whatever lay beneath. It reminded me of looking at an oil sheen in sunlight. I might not know a lot about magic, but even I could deduce that the woman was under some sort of spell. The eyes alone would have been enough, but my nose was giving me additional confirmation as to the woman's identity.

I had found Amy Wells.

Now, I just had to get her out of here before her kidnapper came back. I leapt into the clearing, the noise growing disproportionately larger despite my small amount of movement. Amy didn't react, so I touched her shoulder gently.

"Miss Wells, my name is Fred. I'm a friend of Neil's, and I'm here to help you."

"Neil . . . yeah." Her voice was distant, ungrounded. No wonder she hadn't had the sense to run away. This guy had cast a doozy of a spell on her.

"That's right—Neil. He got us to come save you. We need to hurry, though. I don't know when your abductor will be back."

"Conductor? I'm the . . . conductor." To illustrate, she raised her hands, and the forest exploded with noise. Only after she lowered them did it return to its strange series of sounds. Okay, you're right, that was weird. Weirder still was that there was something about the noises that was nagging at me. It was as though I knew it somehow, like a song lyric you are certain you've heard but you still can't recall.

"No, Miss Wells, your *abductor*. The person who took you from your lab. I need to get you out of here." I reached to pick her up, but the small woman placed a hand on my shoulder.

"Buzz off, narc." I can't tell you the next word she said because it was gibberish to me. What I *can* tell you is that I found myself hurled by some unseen force through the air, my head smashing into a tree with enough force to kill me, had I been human. Still, it rang my bell quite nicely. I had to sit on the ground while my brain swam in order to recover. In my addled state, the nature sounds somehow seemed to grow more cohesive, and suddenly I was struck by a memory from my college days.

I'd had a roommate my freshman year at the dorms. Everyone did, despite their not being adequate room for one person, let alone two. We hadn't gotten along terribly well. I liked to study, and he would consistently blast music on his side of the room. I didn't particularly enjoy it. Then again, I've always been a fan of classics and opera, and I didn't understand what the appeal of it was. Until one day, when I'd come home from a particularly grueling exam to find he'd gone to the communal kitchen and whipped up brownies. As I've said before, I used to have a bit of a weight problem, so I accepted his offer without a second thought. That night, sitting in our dorm, I finally saw why he enjoyed his music so much. In fact, I couldn't get enough of it. The memory was buried down under a combination of time and chemical influences, but now that it had surfaced, everything made a bizarre sort of sense.

"It's Pink Floyd," I announced, more to myself than anyone else.

"Shhhhh," Amy said. "We're at the good part."

My cellphone chirped loudly, earning me a dirty look from the woman with the rainbow eyes, and I flipped it open to an unfamiliar number.

"Fred," Bubba's voice came out low and rough. There was a tremor of relief too, as though he'd been fearful I'd be unable to pick up. Clearly, he was under a lot of stress. "Are you okay? Did you guys get away from those things?"

"I did, though I'm not certain about Albert," I said. "Did you two recover?"

"Yeah, took a few minutes, but we're more or less fine now. We found a payphone in the parking lot after our cellphones got melted. Have you run into any more trouble?"

“Somewhat, though in this case, ‘trouble’ being our missing mage.”

“You found Amy? What about whoever took her?”

“No one took her.” I sighed. “We’ve been wrong the whole time.”

“What do you mean?”

“She isn’t kidnapped. She’s just really, really high.”

8.

THREE HOURS LATER, THE SIX OF US SAT around a table at Taco Bell, watching a woman who couldn't weigh more than a hundred and thirty pounds work her way through a small mountain of Cheesy Gordita Crunches. It had taken that long for Amy to come down enough to effectively communicate, and though her eyes were largely back to normal, I still caught the occasional swirl of color along the edges. She'd explained on the way to the fast food eatery— which she had been insistent we go to—about what happened.

Amy, it seemed, was more than just a talented magic user. She was an accomplished alchemist. She'd been working on a new kind of drug for a very powerful client and had decided to test it on herself. It had worked. Only, since the drug had been calibrated for one much stronger than herself, she'd lost all sense of reality and wandered off into the night. The mosster, the mushmen, and the music had all been her doing, though she only remembered the last one clearly. When asked why on earth she would conjure things like that, her response had been a shrug and the words, "I was suuuuuper messed up."

Neil sat next to her, the fact that she'd never been in any real danger clearly not factoring into his sense of relief or hero worship. She was a pretty woman, but she had over a decade on him, and I was pretty certain his crush was a one-sided affair. Still, she'd managed to turn the kid from an aspiring murderer to a devoted and caring apprentice in only a few weeks, so who was I to argue with results?

Bubba and Richard were putting a serious dent in some food of their own. Both of them were wearing clothes that were closer to scrap cloth than actual attire, the acid having eaten holes in all the available garments. Red splotches of skin still decorated their bodies—the only remaining sign of the eroded flesh they'd suffered—but even that was fading away rapidly. Evidently, healing worked up an appetite, though, since they'd each ordered twenty dollars' worth of food—no small feat at this establishment.

Albert and I were in relatively good shape: a few small holes in our clothing from acid splash we'd failed to notice in our hurried escape. I was also streaked in dirt thanks to Amy blasting me into a tree, and my sweater vest was shredded beyond repair on its back.

I'd thought we might be refused service due to our rough appearance, but, shockingly, we were not the most wrecked group in the Taco Bell that night. Hell, we barely made third place.

"Ohhh man, is that better," Amy said. Usually, these words accompanied the cessation of eating. In her case, they merely came between finishing one taco and unwrapping the next. "Super sorry for all the trouble guys, but I appreciate the ride over."

"I still don't get it," I said, since evidently I was the only one in the dark. "Why would you make something like that in the first place?"

"Fred," Richard said, his tone surprisingly careful for a man of his station. "People of our . . . type are still people. We still have the same desires. We get hungry, we grow tired, we laugh, we love, we hurt. And sometimes, like many other people, there are those among us who yearn for the occasional escape from those feelings."

"Even parahumans want to get high," Amy summed up, swirling down some sugary soda in a few rapid straw sips. "Problem is, most of the usual stuff doesn't work on them. You know how much booze it takes for a therian to get drunk?"

I glanced around nervously. Talking in the open about supernatural things was supposed to be strictly taboo. None of the other patrons seemed to be paying attention to us, though, and since one cluster was debating the viability of robot designs in science fiction worlds while another argued if Lincoln was a time-traveler, I didn't imagine that our conversation would stand out too much.

"A lot," Bubba answered before I could guess. "Goes with the regeneration. I can down an entire bottle of moonshine and only get a light buzz that lasts half an hour."

"Right, exactly, and that's just one hurdle for one type of consumer," Amy said cheerfully. "Zees and Vees and all the other UnDees have their own physical limitations toward tasting sweet release. Through alchemic augmentation, I can create stuff that gets them where they want to go."

"She is brilliant, the best in her field." (Yeah, that was obviously Neil.)

"I guess that makes sense, but it still kind of seems wrong somehow," I said.

"You drink wine," Albert pointed out.

"But because I like the bouquet of flavor."

"Oh. Does that mean you never drank it back before your change?"

Damn. Outfoxed by Albert. If that didn't prove I was in the wrong, nothing would.

"Right, same thing," Amy said. "I provide various means for various people of means. I even comply with all the regulations from the ATF."

"Why do I have a feeling that doesn't stand for Alcohol, Tobacco, and Firearms?"

"'Cause you're right. Alchemy, Thaumatology, and Freshness."

"Freshness?"

"Yeah, I'm not sure that last one wasn't just out of convenience. The other ATF was founded first, and they figured it would be easier to be covert if they worked under a title regular people already knew. Plus, it saved on stationary and uniforms. It *is* still the government, after all."

"This is giving me a headache." I went to set my forehead on the table, then realized exactly where I was and thought better of it.

"I have some stuff back at the lab that can make you forget all about it," Amy offered. "No charge, as apology for all the trouble."

"I'll pass. I'm sorry if I came off as judgmental. I guess I just didn't expect a mage who was mentoring a kid to have gotten involved in something like that."

"Other way around," Amy said, opening the wrapper on her final piece of food. "I got into magic because I got into alchemy. Which I got into because I was into chemistry, which I was learning about because I wanted to get better with botany, which I had taken up studying in an effort to grow some killer weed."

"She really is a prodigy," Richard interjected, having finally finished wolfing down (It's not offensive to use that term. I checked.) a series of Double Decker Tacos. "She got a late start and is still considered more accomplished than mages twice her age. Neil is lucky to have such a teacher."

"Turns out I'm lucky to have such a dedicated apprentice," Amy said, ruffling Neil's hair with the hand that wasn't cramming food in her face. He still got taco sauce streaked on his forehead, but it could have been actual human feces and he wouldn't have cared.

"I guess that's it then," I said. "Everyone is safe, so we can all go home."

"Totally with you there. If I don't whip up a batch of hangover cure, I'm going to be regretting it in the morning. Plus, it sounds like I messed some stuff up while I was tripping."

"On that note, why were there burn marks, blood, and melted glass, along with a destroyed lab?" I asked.

"The drug used a lot of fire magic, and before it was done I had a little accident. As for the rest, I have no idea. Maybe I cast a tornado to cool down. Shouldn't take too long to fix, but, Richard, will you tell Gideon I need a few more days on his order?"

"He will expect adequate compensation for the delay," Richard reminded her.

"Of course he will. Fucking dragons. Tell him I'll add in three extra doses to the order, and to the one after that. If he bitches, you can offer extra on the next one too, no more than that though. A girl's got to eat." Amy illustrated this point by polishing off the last of her food. Neil set a bag of Cinnamon Twists in front of her, which she immediately went to work on.

"That should do it. He'll like the symmetry of the three-by-three offer."

"I'm sorry, are we talking about the Gideon I met tonight? Looks like he's around seven years old?"

"You got it," Amy said. "He's a pain in the ass about the details, but there are worse clients to have than the King of The West."

"The what now?"

"King of The West," Richard said. "He is the highest parahuman authority in our part of the country, answerable only to the Agency. Various types of our kind will appoint their own regional leaders, people with positions like my own. However, they must all be confirmed by Gideon."

"Because he's a dragon?"

"Because he is incredibly powerful, and he is an excellent negotiator. All three of the dragons that assisted in our rebellion demanded vast lands of territory for their aid."

"Our rebellllll—" I stopped as my memory flared up. Krystal had told me something about this over Thanksgiving. America was different from other countries because parahumans had been instrumental in its founding, so much so that they were afforded rights and consideration under the laws. Which meant there was only one plausible rebellion Gideon could have helped with where he would have been able to negotiate such power. "You're saying he was there for the Revolutionary War."

"Very much so. He led a battalion of warriors into some of the key victories, and he is often fond of telling the story of them over and over," Richard explained, clearly a little weary of the tales. I could surmise how a dragon with insane power and innumerable years of experience could make a tiring houseguest.

"Glad to know I made a fool of myself in front of someone so important," I joked. I tried to make it sound lighthearted, but my nerves shone through.

"No need to worry. Gideon is not offended by people cowering in fear of him," Richard assured me. "In fact, he prefers it. Reminds him that he's still got the mojo, even in his current shape."

"No question he does, though, for the life of me, I don't get why someone with all that clout wants to be a kid, or is crashing with one of his subjects," I said. The shadow of some deep pain rippled over Richard's face again, and I decided it was time to move the subject. "I just hope I never give a repeat performance. I'm ready to go home, drink some liquid refreshment, and pass out until the next sunset."

"I'll give you a ride," Bubba said, flashing me a warm grin. He'd been exceptionally cheerful since we met back up, no doubt relieved to know Amy had been found safely. "Look at it this way—at least you have an interesting story to tell Krystal when she gets back."

I chuckled despite myself. "That is true. I bet she thinks all I did while she was gone was sit around and play . . . hey!" I slapped my hand on the table, leaving an accidental dent in its cheap-plastic surface. "I almost forgot."

"What is it?" Richard asked. The whole table leaned in tensely. After a night of constant surprises, they had immediately shifted back into Ready for Anything Mode.

"We still have a game of Scrabble to finish."

"Oooh, can I come? I love that game," Amy said. I was admittedly not overly fond of the woman who had given me a night full of stress and horror, but she had apologized, and it wasn't like she meant to do any harm. Besides, I had spent most of life with very few people to pal around with. It wasn't in me to turn away anyone's advances of friendship.

"Sure," I told her. "The more, the merrier."

"Awesome." She hopped up from the chair and gulped down the last of her drink. "Let me just get some more food to go."

A MONSTER IN THE PEWS

1.

IT WOULD BE LOVELY TO SAY THAT THE stockings were hung by the chimney with care. However, for all the amenities my apartment provided, a fireplace was sadly not one of them. Instead, we used a large wooden stand that I think started its life as a paint easel before Bubba undertook remodeling it. I have to say, it was a far better piece of craftsmanship than anything I could have managed, though Bubba tended to skimp on the more aesthetic details, like paint. And symmetry.

"Hey, Betty Crocker, your cookies are nearly done," Krystal called from the kitchen. No, I don't know why she insisted on telling me this rather than donning an oven mitt and extracting them herself. By this point in our relationship though, it hardly surprised me anymore. I pinned the final stocking—our new friend Amy's—to the makeshift mantle and headed into the kitchen.

"How's the decorating coming?" Krystal asked as I walked in. She sat at the counter polishing off yet another glass of homemade eggnog. At this rate, I'd have to put together another batch before the guests even arrived. Good thing I had the supplies for it. I was nothing if not a contingency planner, but still. It was the principle of the thing.

"Slowly," I told her, taking a look at the crisping chocolate cookies. I'll give her this—she'd been right about their level of doneness. "I could use some help."

"Guess you shouldn't have given Albert the day off, then."

"He put in the form three weeks ago. Besides, he and Neil were going Christmas shopping."

"On December twenty-third? I see that being real productive."

"I suppose all your gift buying is done?"

Krystal turned away, pretending to be sheepish. We'd been dating long enough for me to know better, though. That girl rarely had a sense of shame about anything.

"I might have a few last-minute items to buy. I didn't expect someone to befriend a damn therian Lord and he

King of the West, both of whom protocol demands I make seasonal gifts to."

I was tempted to ask more, but I knew Krystal would just button-up on the details. The agency she worked for, simply known as the Agency among people of my type, was so secret that most of Washington didn't know it existed. It was a job that kept her pretty darn busy, so I was glad they'd given her Christmas off. I pulled open the oven and delicately picked up the trays, setting them on the stovetop to cool before transferring the cookies to wire racks. The heat from the metal trays registered across my naked hands. However, since it wasn't actual fire, there was no damage or pain.

"These should be perfect by the time the guests arrive," I said, checking the clock and realizing with a start that I only had thirty minutes left. That would have been plenty of time normally, but my friends could be a bit disregardful of social convention. There was no telling when they'd start pounding on my reinforced steel door.

"You might need more nog," Krystal informed me, filling up her now empty glass once more.

I scowled at her. "There's a tub of ice cream and a dozen eggs in there. You should have made yourself sick by now. I'll never understand how you eat so much and stay so lean." Krystal and I had both been overweight in high school. Add in social anxiety, and you can see how we'd ended up traveling in similar social circles. My weight loss had come after my change; a liquid diet is quite slimming. As to hers, well, I'd never quite unraveled that mystery. It definitely wasn't her diet, though. That much was quite evident.

"Ancient Chinese secret." She gave me a playful wink that was half-obscured by her blonde hair.

"Says the brown-eyed, white girl." I sighed. "Can you get the new nog started while I go check the lights on the tree?"

"Weeeell, okay. But only because I want to make sure there's enough of this stuff."

I headed back to the living room, momentarily interrupted by the surprise slap to the rear end Krystal had delivered as she moved past me into the kitchen. I shook my head, but there was a smile on my face that she couldn't see. We were a strange couple. I'd be the first to admit that, yet, in a curious way, we seemed to balance one another well. I helped her plan a bit more, and she helped me do things more spontaneously than I normally would.

Halfway through adjusting the lights, I heard a deafening crash come from my kitchen. My first instinct was frustration, and certainty that Krystal had broken my punch bowl. But then I noticed something strange. Vampire hearing is exceptional, so good that I've worked on tuning it out most of the time. As I focused, I realized that there were three other people moving about my apartment . . . and only one of them was breathing.

I dashed into the kitchen before rational thought could kick in—which is likely for the best, since my rational thoughts all center on the principles of running and hiding. The sight that greeted me was far from pleasant. Though I'd reinforced my door after my first few interactions with other parahumans, I had stupidly left my windows unaltered. After all, I lived on the twelfth floor. Who was going to scale a wall and break in?

The answer, it seemed, was the set of men standing in front of an annihilated window. Both were pale and held themselves with a level of balance I was far too familiar with. One wore jeans, a black V-neck shirt, and tattoos covering several hundred pounds of muscle. The other was lean and dressed impeccably in a designer suit, sans tie. He was the one that immediately drew my focus, chiefly because his hand was wrapped around Krystal's neck as she dangled several feet off the floor.

"Good evening, Mr. Fletcher," the one holding Krystal greeted. "Forgive the sudden interruption, but I felt it was high time you and I had a discussion. My name is Quinn Thames, though, given the closeness of our relationship, you may call me Quinn. My burly compatriot here is Beauregard." The muscly man smiled at the mention of his name, confirming my suspicions as he flashed a pair of long fangs where his incisors should be. I really hoped those were extended because he felt like showing them off, and not because of the other . . . possibility, which clearing wasn't feeding. Neither of those two situations ended well for Krystal and me.

"Close relationship?"

"Certainly. There is no greater bond than between a sire and their child."

The trepidation that had been seeping through me catalyzed into outright fear. I'd never seen the vampire who made me. I'd just been attacked one night coming home from the grocery store. When I awoke, there was no note, no guide, no nothing. I'd been changed and cast aside, which, Krystal had eventually explained to me, meant my sire was a sick son of a bitch. In the vampire world, that was the equivalent of tossing a newborn baby in a dumpster.

"I never met my sire," I said carefully.

"No, unfortunately I was called away on unexpected business after your change," Quinn said, ignoring Krystal's attempts to kick him in the head. "However, I had great faith that you would become an exceptional vampire. All the makings were there. You were repressed, weak, and constantly trod upon. I anticipated that I'd return to this city to find you'd nearly drowned it in blood. To say I was disappointed to find that you were coddling around with an agent does not begin to capture my displeasure." He tightened his grip as he spoke, and I could actually hear Krystal's heart slow down a few beats.

"Let her go. She doesn't have anything to do with this."

"That's where you're wrong. You see, Fredrick, I specialize in this. I can sense a simmering bloodlust from across a country. Someone like you only needed the power to strike back against the world, power I provided. Given your spectacular failure, I must surmise that the element which kept you suppressed is this young woman right here." Thankfully, his grip loosened enough to allow airflow again. Krystal tried to mouth something to me, but without her voice, I couldn't understand her.

"What do you want?"

"Finally to the quick of it, eh? I'll make this simple. I want you to fulfill your potential. To that effect, I am going to take Agent Jenkins with me. If you want her back, then come to the church at the corner of Eighteenth and Marigold at midnight. Should you be able to retake her, she's yours. If you fail to come, I'll kill her. And if you come, but then disappoint me again, I'll call it quits on this project and kill you both."

"Whatever you want, let's just do this now," I said. There was no way I could take her back. These guys were real vampires, and I was just a guy in a sweater vest. Still, maybe I could give her the chance to escape. Krystal was an agent; I'd seen her pull off some crazy things before.

I took one step forward and found myself slammed forcefully into the floor. The attack was so hard that it knocked the air out of me. Admittedly, I didn't really need it, but it was still an unpleasant experience. Beauregard looked down at me and flashed another toothsome smile. Even as a new vampire, I could move pretty quickly, and I hadn't even seen him close the gap between us, let alone grab me. Obviously, that didn't bode well.

"Midnight," Quinn called to remind me. "And much like yourself, I greatly value punctuality."

Beauregard gave a swift kick to my torso, and then vanished. By the time I pulled myself up, they were both gone. The only evidence they'd even been real in the first place was the inwardly obliterated window that was letting in the cold December air. Oh, and the fact that Krystal was now nowhere to be seen. With more effort than I'd have expected, I dragged myself to the refrigerator and threw open the door. Grabbing a packet of blood, I bit through the top and began guzzling it down, not even bothering to get myself a glass first. The minor wounds Beauregard had given me were already almost healed, but the last thing I needed was to be running on empty tonight. The extra blood would top me off and finish the recovery.

"Merry Christmas!" My door slammed open to reveal Bubba, dressed in a Santa suit that barely fit him, along with Neil, Albert, and Amy all in tow. They made it three steps inside before the abnormal surroundings registered and their welcoming cheer gave way to sudden concern.

"Guys," I said, finishing up the last of my blood packet. "We have a problem."

2.

BY THE TIME I FINISHED EXPLAINING WHAT happened, the last of my injuries had finished repairing themselves. Albert was hugging his legs on the ground, a look of intense worry on his face. Given Albert's unnaturally cheerful brain chemistry, that was saying quite a lot. Neil, for his part, was digging through book after book, looking up with cursory glances to indicate he was listening, but continuing his research as I spoke. Bubba and Amy both sat quietly, though midway through my story, Amy pulled out a small flask of purple liquid and took a quick nip. Other than that, they both listened intently until I reached the part where they'd entered.

"Sounds like the big one had been draining therians," Bubba said as I fell silent. "As for the guy who grabbed Krystal, we should assume he's even more dangerous. Vampires on therian blood can be wild and hard to control. If he outpaced you by that much, then he's had a lot, and that means this Quinn guy is all the more impressive for keeping him as a lackey."

"There's no trace of any psychic interference or magic," Amy said; her eyes glowed with the same color as the liquid in her flask as she scanned the room. Sometimes it slipped my mind that Neil's mentor wasn't just the girl who spiked our punch with moonshine. She was also a mage regarded as one of the nation's top alchemists. "Quinn must keep his pet beast on a leash of intimidation, which meshes well with Bubba's hypothesis."

"I hope Krystal is okay," Albert whimpered softly. It was so quiet, in fact, that I'm not sure any of the people with human senses heard it. Bubba and I did not fall into that category.

"Krystal will be fine," Bubba assured him. "They don't just hand out agent badges to anyone. That girl could kick a dragon in the teeth if it gave her too much sass." He was doing a good job of sounding sure. However, I was less convinced.

When Krystal and I first reconnected, she'd told me that vampires were big-league monsters. It was strange, since I didn't think of myself as more dangerous than the other things I'd seen her curse out without so much as batting an eye, but it seemed obvious that these two weren't like me. They were real vampires. The way Beauregard had trounced me exemplified that perfectly.

"Bubba, what did you mean when you said he was draining therians?" I asked, as the curious phrasing meshed with my own recollection of Beauregard's physical power.

"Drinking the blood of werecreatures, obviously."

"Oh. Can you smell that in here or something?" I knew from experience that most therians had an adept sense of smell, though my own powerful nostrils weren't picking up anything out of the ordinary. Of course, that didn't mean someone with more experience couldn't notice a subtle cue I'd missed. I got so absorbed in sniffing that it took me a moment to realize everyone save for Albert was staring at me. Even Neil had been drawn out of his rapid page flipping.

"Fred," Amy broached carefully, "Krystal explained to you what makes vampire such dangerous creatures, didn't she?"

"She said we were very powerful. I just assumed she meant the strength, speed, and general difficulty to kill."

Bubba snorted something halfway between a laugh and a grunt of frustration. "That explains a hell of a lot."

"I feel like I'm missing something."

"You're missing a tremendous amount," Neil told me, returning to his books with a shake of his head.

"Be nice," Amy snapped at him. "Not everyone has a teacher to ease them into the parahuman world."

"I'm sorry," Neil mumbled immediately.

"Good." Amy turned to me, pausing only to take a pill from a vitamin bottle and dry swallow it. Given that it had glowed light blue, I highly doubted it was actually what had originally come in the container. The purple glow began fading from her eyes as soon her throat gulped the pill down.

"Fred, are you familiar with the variety of classic vampire mythology?"

"You mean how in some movies they can fly, in others they turn into fog, and in still others they can shape-shift into rats or wolves?"

"Exactly," Amy said. "Most people think the divergence comes from different cultures taking the myth and adding their own spin on it, incorporating aspects they found particularly frightening into an existing monster template. However, that only makes sense if vampires are fictional, which you now know they are not."

It was strange dealing with Amy when she was sober. I could almost feel the weight of her intellect as she processed the information and made it more understandable for me. Her eyes flitted about constantly, absorbing observations and taking in every piece of data around her. No wonder the woman spent so much time in altered mental states. This must be exhausting for her.

"The reason vampire mythology is so convoluted about what they can and can't do is that your kind has an ability unique to their species. Vampires can actually take on the characteristics and powers of other supernatural creatures."

"How do they do that?" Albert asked.

"How else?" Neil said, his tone much kinder than I suspect I would have received. "They drink their blood."

"They . . . we do?" It took considerable self-control to keep my jaw from hanging open in surprise.

"You can," Bubba said. "The stronger the person they drink from, the more potent the effects and the longer it lasts. My kind are their favorite targets, since we give them even greater strength, speed, and senses. If they drink from a powerful enough therian, they even gain the ability to change into that therian's animal for a short while."

"So, we prey on parahumans just as much as regular humans?" Comprehension was shining like the sun, illuminating the strangeness of my encounters with other parahumans in a blinding light of explanation. "That's why so many people have been wary around me. That's why, even in the supernatural world, I was treated with suspicion. They all thought I wanted their blood."

"Not all of us," Bubba said, jerking me back to reality. "Most vampires are assholes, admittedly, but everyone in this room knows you aren't like them."

"This is crazy," I said, walking over to the couch and sitting down. "You're telling me that the people who took Krystal could be capable of anything? Shape-changing, flight, magic—"

"Not magic." Amy was quick to correct me. "Only living creatures can access the mana that flows through the world. Drinking the blood of a mage will give them some resistance to magic, especially from the caster they drank from, but no vampire can actually weave magic."

"Well, that's something I guess."

"It doesn't matter. We can't let you go in after her, anyway," Bubba said. "It's obviously a trap."

"Why trap me? They already had me dead to rights before you got here. Beauregard was so fast he could have gotten my head before I even saw him coming."

"Wrong kind of trap," Neil said, partly closing his tome, but marking the spot with his finger as an impromptu bookmark. "The guy already told you—he doesn't want you dead. He wants you dead*ly*. The goal is to turn you into another pawn, like his guy who drinks therians, or maybe even to make you crazy and unleash you on the city. Either way, I'm sure that whatever is waiting for you at that church is designed to turn you into a monster."

"I think Quinn already accomplished that a year and a half ago," I said.

"No, he didn't." This came from Albert, who managed to uncurl himself and put a reassuring hand on my foot. "Don't say that kind of thing. You gave me a home and a job when I would have been put back to death without them. You risked your freedom to save Bubba and Krystal in Las Vegas. You even helped us find Neil's mentor after he once tried to kill you. You're a good man who happens to be a vampire. We aren't human, but that doesn't make us monsters."

From the mouths of babes. Or, in this case, zombie assistants.

"Thank you, Albert. That was very kind of you." He returned my praise with a lopsided smile, and then scuttled back to the center of the room. I looked back over to Bubba and Amy. "So, what do we do?"

"We call the Agency," Bubba said immediately. "I'm not sure what kind of idiot tries to kidnap one of their people, but I know I've seen powerful beings turn white as a pale moon at the thought of bringin' down the Agency's fury."

"They haven't kept the treaties enforced for over two centuries without having a fair bit of power to swing around," Amy said. "I've heard rumors that if things get bad enough, they even have the right to call on Gideon for assistance."

I swallowed reflexively. Gideon—also known as the King of the West, in case you forgot—a full-blooded dragon that was several millennia old. I'd only met him once, and he'd been shifted into the form of a small child. Even then, he'd scared me so bad I'd gone catatonic.

"There is only one flaw in that plan," Amy continued. "As it stands, an Agency task force might, and I do stress *might*, be able to be rallied in the span of the next hour and make it here in time. While they would doubtlessly bring enough force to take care of two vampires, we must also face the bitter truth that Quinn has shown all the signs of a man who would kill Krystal as soon as he realized we'd decided not to play his game."

"That's suicide," Bubba whispered.

"Undoubtedly. Yet, we have to assume that anyone willing to kidnap an agent is already either too delusional to see the danger or so far gone into madness that they no longer care." Amy touched the side of her head and winced. She reached into one of the countless pockets on her dress and pulled out a small vial that seemed to swirl with green light. A quick motion upended the bottle into her mouth, and a look of tranquility immediately began replacing her pain.

"I agree with Amy," Neil said. "That's why I've been digging through my books. I knew I'd read a spell for something like this. I just had to find it." He reopened the book he'd partially closed, and I realized it was the one I'd seen him with at the LARP, the inherited tome that taught him his first bit of necromancy.

"The simplest solution is just to make him think he got what he wanted. In other words, let's make Fred a monster."

3.

****NOTE: SINCE I WAS NOT PRESENT FOR KRYSTAL'S EXPERIENCE AFTER SHE WAS TAKEN FROM MY APARTMENT, SHE HAS REQUESTED TO TELL THIS PART OF THE STORY IN HER OWN WORDS, RATHER THAN HAVE IT RELAYED. THEREFORE, THE NEXT TWO CHAPTERS WILL RECOUNT A PART OF THE TALE I CANNOT VOUCH FOR, AS I DID NOT WITNESS IT FIRSTHAND.*****

Hello, my name is Krystal, and I'm an agent . . . but you know that. In a world full of vampires, werewolves, fey, dragons, and all the countless other sub-varieties of parahumans we've classified so far, I also tend to stand out as an easy target. Bad guys take one look around a room and decide the blonde gal with the nice cans and the lack of any supernatural heritage markings is the easiest prey there. Some of these bastards are hundreds of years old, and they still haven't learned the lesson of not judging a book by its cover. Well, until they meet me, that is. My point is that, while I was definitely inconvenienced by being kidnapped from my boyfriend's apartment, it was hardly my first rodeo as an abductee.

"Could you put on some music or something?" I was currently chained to an altar in the rear of a formerly abandoned church. Quinn had done a nice job setting the ambiance. Then again, the crazy ones always do; they have a weird flair for getting the décor right. Anyway, all the symbols of Christianity had been wrecked or torn, red markings that looked suspiciously like blood were splattered in key places along the walls, and the corpses of two sizable men—both clearly supernatural given the spots of fur and animal features dispersed across their bodies—hung in the front of the church. Oh, and there were ghouls scattered about, hissing and snapping as they waited for a command.

Ghouls can be split up into two categories: lesser ghouls and greater ghouls (Ghoul Lords). The first are mindless, ravenous, flesh-devouring machines. They have no sense of who they were in life. All they know is an endless, un-abating hunger. Somewhere along the line, people mixed up the mythology of ghouls and zombies. Zombies are like Albert—corpses reanimated for service. It's the ghoul apocalypse people are actually stockpiling for and writing endless fiction about, though a lesser ghoul can't turn a human with its bite. That's a privilege reserved for the Ghoul Lords.

Those guys are far more dangerous, able to command any lesser ghouls they create while still being in possession of their full mental faculties. If not for a vampire's ability to steal powers, Ghoul Lords would likely be near the top of the undead power structure.

Anyway, while the ghouls milling about weren't attacking anything, the sound of their clacking jaws was still annoying as hell, hence my request for music. Plus, I was bored. So sue me.

"Such a brave damsel," Quinn said, perched a few feet away on a decaying pulpit. I'll give him this—the man picked a theme and stuck with it. "There's no need for such demonstrations of bravery. It will not change your fate."

"Uh huh. That's great and all, but I was serious. You guys have obviously been holed up here a while. You've got to have a television or something. I'll take a boom box. The clacking is starting to give me a headache."

Quinn threw back his head and laughed, a rich and elegant tone that had clearly been worked on until it was perfect. Yeah, this was a motherfucker who'd actually practiced his evil laugh.

"I do love the bravado you agents show in the face of certain death," he said, intending it as a compliment, I think. "Sadly, we have no such entertainment devices. Our kind is beyond the need for such petty distractions."

"Buddy, there's an all-vampire group in my department that goes and sings karaoke every Wednesday night. They also took three days off when the last Call of Duty game came out. I happen to know for a fact that Freddy still has an active World of Warcraft account and a giant movie collection. Save the Anne Rice shtick for someone who doesn't work with, and freaking date, your kind."

Quinn had me by the throat in less than a second. Whatever he'd been drinking had imparted a lot of speed. His face contorted into a wild snarl, fangs bared as room-temperature breath swept over me. I could feel the tension in his fingers, the concentrated effort not to crush my throat. He had so much strength it was hard not to, especially because it was obvious how much he would enjoy it. A smart hostage would have started playing nice very quickly.

"Well, now I know you haven't been drinking the blood of a mouthwash monster. That's for damn sure."

A bulge of the eyes, a tremor of the fingers, and I was hurled to the ground.

"Nice try, but I'm afraid I won't be giving in that easily," Quinn said, walking back to his pulpit. "If you were dead when Fred arrived, he might feel compelled to turn tail and flee. I've no intention of letting him go without at least a little effort."

"Right, you think you can turn Freddy into a bloodthirsty monster. Someone didn't get quite enough oxygen to the brain when they changed, did they?"

"Oh, I've come to terms with the fact that I misjudged your boyfriend when I turned him. I'd assumed his spineless nature was a result of his physical frailty, and that a bit of power would allow years of anger and repression to take hold. Imagine my surprise when I came back to discover the man I'd turned really was just a fearful, weak-willed coward. So much so that, even with the powers of a vampire, he still shrinks back from confrontation and challenge."

"You're wrong. Freddy isn't bold, I'll give you that, and, yeah, his first instinct is usually to take cover, but he's also the kind of man who always does his best when the chips are down. I've seen him face his fear several times to help people he barely knew."

"So I've heard. Which is what I'm counting on," Quinn said. "You see, I know that he is currently trafficking in the company of a necromancer. Once upon a time, that was my specialty as well. Dedicated student that Neil is, I'm sure he's uncovered the spell of *Mortis Invictus* by now. It's a charming little ritual that taps into an undead creature's true potential. All our powers are augmented tenfold."

"And let me guess—it also amplifies your bloodlust proportionally?"

"As well as our aggression. Though, the spell's description leaves out those choice tidbits. How did you know?"

"Because, otherwise, you wouldn't be so cheerful about the possibility of a super-vampire knocking on your door. Though, I'm still not sure how you win if you temporarily turn Fred crazy and he tears your head off."

"I'll be fine. Thank you for the concern. That's what the ghouls are for. And while the physical effects of Mortis Invictus are temporary, opening the door to that side of the mind is something that can never truly be undone. Add in the guilt over his inability to save you, and the rage from when I kill the rest of your friends—assuming he doesn't gut them himself the minute the spell takes hold—and I suspect dear Fredrick will be a wild beast before New Year's."

"Hoo boy. This night is not going to end well for you." I should have been more concerned. Quinn was crazy, but the kind of crazy that thought well ahead. Luckily, I knew what he hadn't noticed. I'd mouthed a message to Fred not to follow me, because I would be fine. Coupled with his own natural reticence, there was no way he was going to come try and save the day, so there would be no need to cast some stupid undead steroid spell. Still, it had been a good plan. I'd have to make sure to kill Quinn first when this came to a head. Guys like him usually had escape plans to enact, if given half a chance.

"Keep telling yourself that," he said.

I opened my mouth to pop off another reply, but a familiar sputtering engine-cough slammed my jaw shut in surprise. Bubba's truck was barreling down the street, which meant those damned idiots were going to try and play cavalry despite all basic logic. I was an agent, for hell's sake. Did they really think I couldn't deal with a Bond-villain wannabe who happened to sport fangs?

"Sounds like the fun will be starting soon." Quinn stationed himself at the pulpit in a somber, expectant pose. We were both tense, waiting for the crunch of brakes and sound of approaching footsteps. In that anticipation, we were both sorely mistaken.

The front of the truck smashed through the partially-rotted wood doors, crashing through the first two rows of pews and rolling over several ghouls before coming to a stop. The driver's door flew off (and I do mean "flew"), as it was thrown effortlessly against the wall by a pair of pale hands. With aching slowness, the driver emerged from the truck's cab, moving like a snake as it danced around a mongoose.

His glasses were gone, revealing a pair of eyes that were throbbing with a dark red light. The normally fastidiously-fastened collar had been left open, blood staining the fabric along with his mouth, throat, and chest. I really didn't want to think about where all that blood had come from. Strangely, the sweater vest still clung tightly to his torso, adding a surreal element of familiarity to the monster that had formerly been my boyfriend. His fangs were fully extended, and he greeted the room with a hissing snarl.

"Fuck," I whispered. Things had just gotten much more complicated.

4.

FREDDY, OR WHATEVER REMAINED OF HIM in the red-eyed monster staring at us from across the church, let out a snarl and smashed his hand through the nearest pew. Splinters went flying, tearing through a few of the nearby ghouls, much to their confusion. Those things would have been on Freddy like drunks on an unguarded bar tap if he'd had a heartbeat, but whatever supernatural hunger drove them didn't crave undead flesh. The working theory was that this instinct was woven into the magic that animated them, since, without it, creating ghouls would result in a wild feeding frenzy on one another. They would still attack if they were commanded to, though I wasn't entirely sure who was pulling their strings. They were definitely under someone's control. That much was obvious. Otherwise, they'd have tried to devour me as soon as they caught a whiff of my scent, and this whole ugly incident would have been over already.

Quinn let out a low whistle. "That necromancer had some serious skill. This is quite a transformation. Pity, I imagine at least some of that blood staining your boyfriend's neck belongs to the would-be magician. Or should I say 'belonged'?"

That line was probably already cliché in whatever century this dick was turned, yet for some reason, it got under my skin. Probably because I had already had the same thought moments before. Who all had been coming to the party? Nick, Bubba, Albert, and Amy. Amy or Bubba might have been able to fight Freddy off, but if he'd drank from one of them first, the others would have been fucked. My stomach turned the longer I stared at the red streaks on Freddy's skin and clothes. Stupid idiot. Why hadn't he just stayed away?

"Hey, Quinn," I called, working hard to keep my more fearful emotions off my face. The only thing he was allowed to see was my anger, and I had plenty of that to spare. "When this is all over, I'm going to tear your limbs off and leave you with your dick exposed to sunlight. Then I'm going to get a mage that can heal you and repeat the process until I get bored."

He glared at me. I think he imagined I would have started begging for my life by now. I probably didn't fit into his expectations for how this was supposed to work. Welcome to the Krystal Disappointment Club, asshole. Tell my father and ex-fiancé "hi" at the next meeting.

"I've had enough of your mouth," Quinn said at last. "I was going to kill you first, but I think I'll let you live a bit longer, while we subdue the man you seem to care so deeply for." He raised his hands, the sleeve on his right arm falling back enough to reveal an ornate bracelet giving off a dark glow. At least that explained the ghouls. Undead can't cast magic, but they could use enchanted items, if they knew how. "Ghouls, Beauregard, put our guest in more of a listening mood."

Just like that, the murder switch in the ghouls' brains was clicked on, and they began rushing toward Freddy. I noticed the hulking form of Beauregard moving forward as well, but he did so at a much more casual pace. Thankfully, Freddy saw all of this too, though it seemed his sense of priorities was different. Rather than swatting at the ghouls bearing down on him, Freddy did what he'd always done best. He jumped, dodged, and evaded. He ran like hell. The only difference in this and the Freddy I'd known since high school, the one I'd started to . . . have feelings for, the one I'd been with only hours earlier, was that this Freddy didn't try to get away from danger. Oh, he was running, all right, running straight at Quinn.

This, far more than the previous command, seemed to kick Beauregard into high gear. The large vampire clearly hadn't been expecting Freddy to make a beeline for his boss. It took him so long to correct his course, though, that Freddy was able to make it halfway to the pulpit. Then again, Beauregard didn't intercept Freddy so much as crash into him, so the progress was definitely balanced with some setback.

Freddy surprised all of us, though. Instead of just collapsing like he had in his apartment, he flipped over the shoulder cracking into him and landed on his feet on the other side. As soon as his loafers—oh, sweet heaven, he was still wearing those, wasn't he? Anyway, as soon as his loafers touched the ground, he was off again, fangs glinting in the light as he snapped furiously. Whatever was driving him along, it seemed to be single-mindedly set on Quinn.

Beauregard was surprised by his opponent's gymnastic talents, but that wasn't enough to make him forget what his job was. With more grace than a man his size had any right possessing, he spun around and tried to grab Freddy by the arm. It was unsuccessful, though barely. The magic amping up Freddy was impressive, no doubt about it, but I could see why Quinn was relatively unconcerned. If his lackey had enough skill and power to keep up with Freddy, then the mastermind almost certainly did.

A few more failed swipes, a few more frantic steps forward, and Freddy was nearly within spitting distance of his goal. Unfortunately, that was because Beauregard got tired of pawing at him and took it to the next level. He surged forward, wrapping Freddy in a powerful hug that no amount of nimble movement was going to get out of, and then threw the two of them to the ground. They met the concrete with a mighty crunch, and for a moment, the world was silent. Had either of them been living, the sounds of heavy breathing would have filled the air. Instead, there was only the smug satisfaction practically echoing from Quinn, the clacking jaws of the pursuing ghouls, and a sullen quiet from the vampire pinned only a few feet away. He'd made it so close, though I had no idea what he'd thought would happen if he—

"NOW!" Freddy yelled, startling everyone in the room with a sentient mind. Well, everyone we'd all known about.

"*Ectorim Novendum, Bicradalio*!" The words were familiar, though not so much that I could place them. The voice, on the other hand, I knew in an instant. Neil's spell echoed through the church, the force in his voice so strong I thought it was going to knock the dust from the rafters. I felt a soft pulse of magic from nearby—again, familiar in a way I couldn't quite place. As the words faded, I realized the world had gone silent again, but this time it was different.

This time, the world had frozen. The ghouls stood, as unmoving as fucked-up wax figures and at least twice as ugly. Quinn was a statue, which made the look of surprise on his face all the more appropriate. Beauregard was stuck as well, his head halfway up as he twisted his eyes to find the source of the voice. I followed his eyes to find a small figure climbing out of the the truck's bed, chucking an enormous blanket back into the vehicle's depths.

"Neil?"

"Hey, Krystal," he called, giving me a wave. For a young man surrounded by ghouls, he seemed extraordinarily unconcerned.

I noticed one more area of movement, then; this one far more relevant to my situation. Freddy had peeled off the frozen form of Beauregard and was approaching my spot near the altar. His eyes still glowed with that strange red light, but there was something different in the way he was moving.

"Freddy? You okay in there?"

He reached down and pulled apart my chains with a small grunt of effort.

"No, I'm not okay," he said, his voice even and normal despite the strange glowing eyes and crazy-ass antics. "I was halfway here when I realized that, in all the chaos, I forgot to take the roast out of the oven. It's going to be ruined by the time we get back."

I grabbed that wuss by the shirt collar, pulled him close, and gave him a kiss that would make the dead stand up in their graves.

Sex pun abso-fucking-lutely intended.

5.

*****NOTE: HERE, SINCE I WAS ON THE SCENE ONCE MORE, IT ONLY SEEMS APPROPRIATE THAT I RESUME THE DUTY OF RECOUNTING THE INCIDENT. THOUGH I'D LIKE TO THANK KRYSTAL FOR THAT . . . COLORFUL RENDITION OF WHAT WENT ON BEFORE I ARRIVED.*****

When Krystal finally let me go, which I was both happy and sad to have happen, the joy of seeing me not a monster was at last overcome with her need to understand just what the hell was going on. I could hardly blame her for that. It was a trait that likely made her successful in her career. Still, it was nice to—for once—know something that she didn't, and I was half-tempted to savor the moment. Then I noticed the sternness in her eyes and remembered that I was not only helping my girlfriend to her feet, I was helping an agent. In this situation, I had no doubt which trumped the other.

"Spill," Krystal said, once she was standing. "What the hell was all that? And why aren't you some crazy, blood-hungry monster?"

"Neil proposed a spell that would have amplified my vampiric abilities by several degrees, but we ultimately decided against it. Even though he said it would have made me strong enough to stand against them, I had to raise the point that I would still be . . . well . . . me. I'm not good at conflict, and definitely not good enough to overcome two men who seemed to relish it, even with a strength boost. He then suggested altering the ritual to dull my human sensibilities, but when he and Amy looked it over to see if that was even viable, they realized that a big component of the spell was already mind altering. From there, Amy put together the working theory that Quinn had known I had a necromancer as a friend and was counting on us utilizing the spell to come save you."

Krystal rubbed her ankles where she'd been bound, and then stood to her full height. She surveyed the room carefully, checking for threats. There were none she could discern, or at least, none I could discern her discerning. Still, she walked over to Quinn and began to test his paralysis, or at least, that was what I presumed she was doing by thumping him in the eye.

"So, you didn't use Mortis Invictus. Then what was all of" —she paused her pestering of Quinn to gesture at the wrecked church and the frozen ghouls—"this?"

"Once we knew what they were expecting, it seemed like we might be able to use it to our advantage. Amy cast a spell to give me the scary eyes. A little creative tailoring and some blood from my fridge completed the image of a magically-altered brute."

"Uh huh, but why?"

I held up my wrist to show her a tiny metal charm. "Amy taught Neil about talismans a while back. She removed his collar, so he was able to use it to cast that undead freezing spell he used at the LARP from wherever the talisman was located. Evidently, with stronger vampires, you need proximity to be effective. Good thing the ghouls were weak enough to be taken at a distance. We didn't know they'd be here."

"That's great, but what about—"

"All the dodging?" I said, rushing over her question. It was poor etiquette, but I was excited. I'd never really gotten to do the big reveal before. "Amy gave me a potion that enhanced my speed, perception, and dodging. She calls it 'cat's dexterity,' or something like that. Turns out, she makes more than just drugs for dragons."

"Fred," she said, taking in a long sigh that told me she was trying not to let her frustration get the better of her. I could have guessed, just from her choice of word, that she was serious. I couldn't remember the last time she called me something other than "Freddy." "You aren't getting it. My question is not how you all managed this little coup—it's why you bothered in the first place." She turned away from Quinn, evidently satisfied that he was truly held. His eyes lingered on her, somehow still managing to convey a sense of fury despite their unmoving status.

"I told you not to come," she said. "I mouthed it at you when they were pulling me away."

"I didn't catch that."

"Fine, but you still should have known not to bother. I'm an agent, dammit, and I know you're still learning what that means, but I'd hoped you'd have figured out by now that it's a title given to people who can take care of themselves. Yes, I have some limitations that let me get captured more easily than others. I've been doing this for a long time, though. I survived just fine without someone riding in to play cowboy and save me from the train tracks."

"I think you sort of mixed genres there. Dudley Do Right did the train-track thing." I knew it wouldn't help un-rile her. I just wasn't sure what else to say. Krystal was the Type B Personality in our relationship. I so rarely saw her serious, even in dangerous situations, that I wasn't used to calming *her* down.

"It doesn't matter." She thrust a finger in Quinn's face, her exposed flesh mere inches from his mouth. "*This* is not a threat to me. He is an inconvenience. He is a dinner-plan wrecker. He is an apartment smasher. But that's all. He's an annoyance. To the rest of you, he is a very deadly opponent. You should have let me handle my own business."

"I'm sorry. I didn't know. I . . . I just didn't want anything to happen to you."

We were interrupted by sounds from the front of the church. A glance showed us that Amy, Bubba, and Albert had arrived and were trying to extricate Bubba's truck from the pews smashed beneath it. They'd followed at a distance during the front-door-smashing bit. Neil was only along so he could cast his spell, and Amy had only consented to letting her apprentice do that much after laying several protection spells atop him. Between the magic and the armored blanket—an item which none of us had wanted to ask Bubba why he kept on hand—the amateur necromancer was probably safer than I was during the drive.

"You brought the rest of the crew?"

"They insisted. We care about you, Krystal. None of us was comfortable with sitting around while two vampires did who-knew-what to you. When we first met, you told me that vampires were only assigned to really powerful agents, and you've never mentioned dealing with one."

"That isn't because they can kill me. It's just because subduing them isn't my specialty."

"I didn't know that. Neither did they. We were worried about you, and no matter how mad you get, I'm afraid none of us is going to tell you we regret what we did tonight, because you're standing here safe and sound. Maybe we were wrong, but we were the sort of wrong that ends with getting our friend back, and I think I speak for everyone when I say we can make peace with that." Despite my brave words, I took a slight step back and braced tentatively. Krystal was a passionate woman; I was therefore prepared to receive an emotional, if not violent, response.

She let out a long breath and ran her fingers through her hair. After a moment, she walked back over to me and placed her arms around my shoulders. "I know, Freddy. I realize it was well intentioned. This is just a touchy topic for me. I'm a little prone to overreaction." She leaned in and gave me a kiss, not like the one she had when she saw me, but one that still would have taken my breath away if I'd had any. Once she pulled away, she continued talking.

"I'm serious about this, though. You and the Scooby Doo crew *have* to rein in any cavalry impulses when my safety is all that's on the line. Trust that I can handle myself in situations like this, especially against pissants like Qui—"

Later on, I'd be able to reconstruct the memory, noticing what my vampire eyes had seen and my distracted brain had missed. The hot spray of her blood splashed across my face as her throat disappeared. It had happened in an instant, a pale hand reaching around from behind her, clutching her too-tan-for-the-season throat, and ripping it out. But that understanding would come later down the line. In that moment, all I felt was the sticky spurt of blood strike my face. All I heard was the moist gurgling of her next words oozing out of her now exposed throat. All I saw was her fall sideways and flop to the ground, lifeless save only for an occasional twitch.

Once she was gone, I got a great view of Quinn, movements clearly unhindered and right hand coated in blood.

"I told you to stop talking," he said, eyes on her body as the intermittent jerking began to slow. "But, like all women, you just didn't know when to shut up."

6.

BEFORE THE LAST REVERBERATIONS OF HIS words had finished bouncing off the church's wall, Quinn had closed the meager gap between us and hurled me back several feet. I was able to land on my feet thanks to Amy's potion, but they'd no sooner touched the ground than Quinn was there, delivering a quick blow that knocked me to the ground and shattered the bones in my shoulder.

"Did you think the curse of some apprentice was going to be enough to hold me? I once commanded the magical forces with my own will. The first thing I did upon turning was set up precautions against such manipulations." He reached down and plucked me from the ground, holding me with the hand still caked in Krystal's blood. The smell was nauseating, which was strange in itself. Even if I loved the woman it came from, blood should still smell like blood. If Quinn noticed the strange scent, he didn't seem to care.

A jerk of his wrist smashed me into the solid, wooden wall behind me. His grip tightened, though it was more symbolic than painful. I wasn't going to be suffocated anytime soon. Under different circumstances, I might have been thankful for that fact. I kicked futilely. He didn't even seem to register the impacts against his torso. Switching tactics, I clawed at the wrist pinning me to the wall, but even my undead nails couldn't so much as scratch his flesh. If Beauregard had been dense, then Quinn was like living dark matter.

"You couldn't even make yourself useful at the end," Quinn lectured. Over his shoulder, I saw a sight that gave me the barest flicker of hope. Bubba had shifted, and now a large pony was barreling toward us, followed some distance behind by Amy, Albert, and Neil. Maybe together, the four of us could—

"Beauregard," Quinn commanded. "Kill the rest of them." As he spoke, a strange symbol flickered across his throat, too complex and too brief for me to make it out clearly. Whatever it was, it evidently gave his words more weight than Neil's spell, since the larger vampire rose and turned to meet the impending mini-steed. The two collided with a sonorous crash, and then Bubba was airborne as Beauregard hurled him away with, apparently, little effort.

My struggling grew more frantic. I tried every move I could remember from a life of being bullied and held down. Wriggling, kicking, scratching, even trying to poke him in the eyes. None of it loosened his grip in the slightest.

"No, Fred, no happy escape or quick death for you. It's clear I made a mistake in turning you . . . I'll own that failure. But you must be punished for disappointing me. So, before I tear your head from your body and leave it out for daylight to char, you're going to watch me turn all your precious friends into bloody chunks. Just like I did to your girlfriend."

If I could have begged, or pleaded, or whimpered, I'll freely admit that I would have. But sadly, even the undead, or at least my type of undead, need vocal cords to make coherent sound. Instead, I was forced to flounder silently as Beauregard turned his attention to my more vulnerable friends. There was nothing I could do. I was stuck. We were all going to die. And just when life had stopped being so lonely. (Oh, don't get technical with it. You know I mean in a general sense rather than referring to being actually alive.)

That's when history repeated itself.

One moment I was stuck there, watching death, shaped like a roided-up vampire, draw inevitably closer to my friends. The next, I was falling to the ground. I surprised myself by landing on my feet again, but then remembered Amy's potion was still in effect. I had all of a half-second to appreciate that sense of freedom before Quinn's bloodcurdling screams began crashing against my ears.

He was hollering in pain, the likes of which I hope I die (the permanent kind) long before experiencing. The stump at this shoulder where his right arm had been was leaking blood at a rapid pace, though substantially slower than a living heart would be causing it to spurt. I cast my eyes about for the missing appendage, finding it with little difficulty. For one thing, it was on fire, turning to ash at an astonishing rate.

For another, it was clutched in Krystal's hands.

Well, sort of. Her hands were now about half-claw—dark, twisting things that extended from her middle knuckle and stretched much further than her normal digits. Her skin seemed to be shifting, like something beneath it was rearranging itself. The blonde hair I'd come to know so well turned blood red midway down its length before ending with a fire red at the tips. That last part isn't creative description, either; the tips of her hair were literally burning. It was a strange effect, but at least it matched the mini-infernos blazing where her eyes used to be.

"Awww, does the big, bad vampire miss his arm?" Her voice was still partly hers, yet there was another tone coming out in concert with it. The second voice sounded like the screams of a thousand children waking from nightmares, only to find their families slaughtered around them. If I were still capable of bowel movements, I'm certain I would have soiled my pants upon hearing it.

She blurred for a moment. Then she was next to Quinn, her movements so fast not even my eyes could track them. Casually, she held up the flaming remains of his arm. A wide—too wide, in fact—smile drew across her face, revealing teeth serrated and sharp and too many rows deep. There was a slight surge, and the arm crumbled to the ground, nothing more than flakes of ash.

"I told you I would tear off your limbs. Did you think I was bluffing? Did you imagine it was really that easy to kill an agent?" Krystal ran a claw along his face. Quinn was either too terrified or in too much pain to react. Where it touched, his seemingly invincible skin split open with a faint sizzling and a puff of smoke. "You tried to kill me, which means I'm well within my rights to take you apart in any way I see fit. You also tried to kill my friends, which means I'm going to get a tremendous amount of joy from doing just that."

"Krystal? Is that . . . what's going on?"

"Sorry, honey," she said. She didn't move her head, but she might have been looking at me. With the blazes in her sockets, it was hard to track her vision. "I guess I have some explaining to do, but it will have to wait until after."

I didn't need to ask what "after" meant, and I am certain Quinn didn't either. He was finally getting a grip on himself, marshaling some control over the pain, which seemed to be getting rapidly replaced by panic. Fortunately for him, we'd all forgotten that he wasn't there all by himself.

Beauregard leapt on Krystal's back from ten feet away, no doubt expecting to send the slender-framed woman sprawling as he had the rest of us. In that regard, he was in for a very unpleasant surprise. Krystal barely twitched at the impact, reaching up and behind her at an angle that should have been impossible for even the lithest gymnast, and sank her claws into his exposed flesh. She ripped him off and spun around, her free hand running across his torso and shredding his skin like wet toilet paper.

"I appreciate your dedication, but it would have been wiser to learn how to pick your battles when you had the chance. Still, you were just under orders, so I guess there's no need to be cruel about this."

With a single swipe of her hand-claw, Beauregard's head toppled from his shoulder, beginning to burn before it even thumped off the dirty carpet. His body was starting to smolder as well, so Krystal released her grip on it and let it tumble away. With the lackey finished, she turned her attention back to the true subject of her wrath.

Only it was nowhere to be found. In the ten seconds Beauregard had diverted our attention, Quinn had somehow managed to scramble away. I sniffed the air, thinking that perhaps I could pick up the scent of his blood since he was injured. The air was thick with the smell, all right, but it didn't extend beyond us. Whatever Quinn had used to vanish, it had somehow covered his tracks. *Very* effectively.

"And that's why I hate his type," Krystal mumbled. "They always have escape plans." She turned to me, and I put all my effort into not letting out a yelp of terror. "Come on. Let's go check on everyone."

I complied, following immediately—partially out of genuine concern, and partially out of overwhelming fear.

7.

SEVERAL HOURS, A LONG PHONE CALL, AND many assurances to our friends later, Krystal and I were finally holed up—just in time to avoid the coming sun. We were at her place (which I had never been to), since mine currently had a broken window and a hole in the brick where it had once resided. For most people, that was an inconvenience, but obviously, the sun would do more to me than leave a tan. Thankfully, Bubba had promised he could get it at least quasi-repaired before the next dawn, so I would keep my tenure as a houseguest to a minimum.

Her domicile was surprisingly elegant, with smooth marble floors and modern décor, as well as stainless steel appliances. She'd only been in town for a month, so I concluded that everything was brand new. I hadn't realized agents made so much money. Evidently, there were a multitude of things I wasn't aware of, though at least one of those was about to change.

I settled into a comfortable chair, glass of a pinot noir in hand, and readied myself. Krystal plopped into an opposing seat and cracked open one of her beers. She was almost completely back to normal, though the tips of her hair were still tinged with crimson. Her eyes—her real eyes, thankfully—were back to their usual brown, though the bags beneath them spoke to how exhausting her endeavor had been. I strengthened my resolve; this was not a time for pity. Krystal had promised me some answers once we were safe, and now that the night was done and her call with the home office was completed, the time had come to collect.

"So," I probed gently. "You turn into a fire monster."

"Sort of," she said, pausing to take a long sip from her beer. "It's complicated. Are you really sure you want to hear this? You've adjusted well to the parahuman world, but there's still a lot you don't know. Stuff you are probably much happier not knowing. Vampires can be tough bastards, but they are far from the baddest guys on the block."

"I noticed. Look, if you'd asked me last night, I'd have probably declined. However, after today, I think not knowing is more dangerous than dealing with the knowledge that boogeymen might be under my bed."

"Don't be silly. Boogeymen don't prey on undead," Krystal said.

"You're stalling."

"Yes, I am." She took another sip of beer, this one much deeper than the first. "Devil."

"Beg pardon?"

"It's not a fire monster. It's a devil. A being of Hell significantly more powerful than mere demons. Most of our more religious agents believe they were the angels that fell in Lucifer's rebellion, but we're never seen defendable evidence of that being the case. The more secular agents see Hell as a dimension that runs close to ours, and devils as beings at the top of its food chain."

"Okay, and you're, what, part devil?"

Krystal snorted. "Heck no, only demons can crossbreed. Devils are too powerful. No, I'm significantly more complicated. Do you remember my mother?"

I nodded. "Nice woman. Sold real estate."

"She got cancer in my first year of college."

"I'm so sorry."

Krystal waved me off. "It was a long time ago. I'm okay. Point is that, before I was a sophomore, she was gone. Then, on Christmas break of that year, I got into a car accident. It was bad. I was T-boned against a concrete barrier. Steering column went through my chest and crushed my heart. I died."

I stayed silent as she spoke, watching her carefully. Krystal was never an overly emotional person, but as she recounted her own death, it was clear she was fighting back a full, sobbing breakdown. Strangely, on this account, I could relate.

"I died," she repeated. "That's when I felt this . . . thing bubble up from inside me. I woke up like you saw me tonight and carved my way out of the car, out of the world I thought I'd known, and out of my nice, normal life." A quick motion killed her beer, and then she walked over to the fridge for another. I waited until the top was popped before speaking.

"I'm sorry, but I still don't really understand what you are."

"That's okay. There's not many of my kind, so we don't get a lot of press. Sometimes, very rarely, a devil will break into our plane. When they do, it's a horrific event, more damage than you can even imagine. Killing them is damn near impossible. It's only been accomplished twice in known history, and the parahuman history books go back much farther than the regular ones. There are other ways to deal with them, though. Banishing, if you can swing it. Sometimes, they'll go back on their own if properly bribed. And then there's the method relevant to our discussion: imprisonment."

"I have a feeling you aren't going to tell me you send them to Alcatraz." I took a gulp of my wine. It wouldn't get me drunk, but the motion reassured me nonetheless.

"There's a ritual that can be used. Binds them, seals them, holds them. You need a virgin girl and a powerful mage to do it. It . . . well, it gets sort of technical here, and I don't even have the magic chops to really understand it all, but the easiest way to say it is that the devil is sealed in a soul and bound by the blood. The spell is tied to that person's blood, the circulatory system acting as a constant prayer wheel, every pump of the heart reinforcing the cage."

"So, wait, you were—"

"No. God no. One of my ancestors, *waaaay* back when. The curse, or duty, or whatever you call it, is passed down along the bloodline. When a woman has a daughter, the onus of the spell begins to transfer. It completes itself when the girl hits puberty. From that point on, if the girl dies, well . . . what you saw tonight happens. The devil that's bound in me shares my fate. If I die, it will kill him too. So until I bear a child, it will always come out like that to revive me."

"Why didn't it help your mother then?"

"She'd already had me. If I had a daughter, I would lose its protection the minute she hit puberty. Mom never died before having me, so she never knew about any of this. I don't think any of my recent family did."

"I see. Then it seems like the easiest way out would be to not have children and let your physical clock run out. Surely, it can't revive you when you die of old age."

"You wouldn't believe what it can do," Krystal told me, her eyes darting to the wall, though I sincerely doubt that is what she was seeing. "I won't get old. I won't get sick. I'll be like this until I pass on the curse."

"Wow." Okay, not exactly eloquent, but I'd like to see how you deal with that sort of revelation. "That is some heavy stuff. I guess your agency filled you in on everything?"

Krystal bobbed her head. "They found me after the wreck, gave me answers and counseling, and then eventually offered me a job." Her eyes came back to me and a small smile graced her lips. "I'm not as powerful as most people in my field, though I do get a few perks from my condition. A little bit strong, a little bit fast, a metabolism that helped me shed all that high school fat, plus a hefty resistance to certain magics. My ace in the death hole is what qualifies me for this job, though, and that's the one part that almost makes all of the rest worthwhile."

"I'm glad you found a way to make it into a good thing," I told her. "Honestly, you seem much happier than you ever did when we were both normal."

"Thanks. You too."

I didn't even imagine debating her on that point. My life and my unlife couldn't have been more different in terms of enjoyability.

"Look, Freddy, maybe we rushed into this thing. There's a reason people in my career tend to date co-workers. Our lives are dangerous by their very nature, and sometimes that danger spills over onto the people near and dear to us."

"Oh please, don't even try to play that card. If you recall, those men broke into *my* apartment, looking to make *my* life more problematic. You were collateral damage, and if you hadn't been there, then they almost certainly would have done the same thing using Albert, or Amy, or someone who doesn't have a get-out-of-death-free card."

"Point taken. They were after you . . . this time. I've had more jumpings and break-ins than you can imagine, though. Do you know why you've never been to my place before? Because I don't know if it's being watched yet. It will be eventually, and I didn't want you on anyone's radar."

"We aren't worried about that anymore?"

"Not with Quinn the Psycho on the loose. He'll blab to anyone who wants to listen. Agents aren't universally reviled, but that doesn't mean we don't have enemies. Sooner or later, being with me will mean trouble for you."

"Because I would handle myself so well without your protection."

"I think you'd do better than you realize. We'd line up protection for you, anyway. Sadly, this is far from the first time an agent has hit this situation."

"I see." I finished off my wine and tried to keep the sweeping sense of sadness off my face. "I have to say, as far as break-up excuses go, this is better than 'it's not you, it's me,' but only marginally."

"Wait, I thought you'd want to break up with me," she said, her eyebrows rising significantly. "I just finished telling you I'm a flesh cage for a devil."

"I'm an undead blood-drinker," I pointed out.

"Being with me will put you in danger."

"Tonight tells us that vice versa could also be true."

"Freddy, this life, it isn't for everyone. I know you. I know how you like to live. You think these past two months are as bad as it gets? You've barely gotten past the tip of the iceberg, and the longer we're together, the harder it's going to be to get your peace and quiet back."

I set my wine glass on the table and rose to my feet. Krystal mimicked my motions, I suspect to give me a final embrace before I walked out the door. Instead, I took her face in my hands and pulled it upward so it faced mine.

"I spent my whole life being very cautious and very safe, and it ended with me very dead under a dumpster. Perhaps I'm not the sort who can overhaul his entire personality with one death. However, I have at least learned enough to no longer shy away from something that has made my world, while more dangerous, also impossibly more worth being in." With that, I kissed her—an awkward peck far less gallant than I'd been hoping for. But, as I'd admitted, I am not the sort to easily change. Perhaps suaveness will come to me in another hundred years.

"I'll give you this," Krystal said once we parted, "you sure impressed me tonight. I get all the magic helping you dodge and making you look scary. But how did you pull off the snarling and insanity act?"

"If you'll recall, I'm an ardent fan of cinema and theatre. I even auditioned for our high school's theatre program."

"Yeah, and then you got so nervous you threw up midway through your monologue," Krystal added. "I will say, though, the first half was pretty good at least."

"Well, there's your answer."

"Where's my answer?"

"In what you said. I vomited every time I tried to act. A physical impulse that vampires don't have."

"Wait, so you're saying the reason you were able to put on that performance is because vampires don't puke?" Krystal's already impressive grin collapsed into a din of laughter which grew increasingly hard to interpret as being kindly meant the longer it wore on.

"I don't see what's so funny."

"Of course you don't," she managed to choke out between guffaws. "Oh, Freddy, honey, you really are one of a kind." She stifled her laughter long enough to pull me in for her own show of affection—this one far more charismatically executed than my own.

Someday, I'd get the moves down. Someday, I'd be the cool, action-star type of guy who could make a moment his own. Someday, I would figure all of this stuff out.

Until then, at least there's no shortage of time to practice.

ABOUT DREW

Drew Hayes is an aspiring author from Texas who has written several books and found the gumption to publish a few (so far). He graduated from Texas Tech with a B.A. in English, because evidently he's not familiar with what the term "employable" means. Drew has been called one of the most profound, prolific, and talented authors of his generation, but a table full of drunks will say almost anything when offered a round of free shots. Drew feels kind of like a D-bag writing about himself in the third person like this. He does appreciate that you're still reading, though.

Drew would like to sit down and have a beer with you. Or a cocktail. He's not here to judge your preferences. Drew is terrible at being serious, and has no real idea what a snippet biography is meant to convey anyway. Drew thinks you are awesome just the way you are. That part, he meant. Drew is off to go high-five random people, because who doesn't love a good high-five? No one, that's who.

Printed in the USA
CPSIA information can be obtained
at www.ICGtesting.com
LVHW091925050624
782385LV00004B/581